Praise [...]
Mi[...]

"Simon Rich's *Miracle Workers* is divinely funny."
—Elissa Schappell, *Vanity Fair*

"Hilarious and touching.... Rich is crazy good at hysterical, sharp dialogue. But the bonus here is that his head is matched by his heart. Rich lends the potentially gimmicky story real emotional heft and avoids condescending to his characters (or readers). At its best, *Miracle Workers* reads like a screenplay for a film that might sit comfortably beside Woody Allen's early absurd works in a Netflix queue."
—Ray Rahman, *Entertainment Weekly*

"Like Douglas Adams in *The Hitchhiker's Guide to the Galaxy,* Rich drags heaven down to Earth.... Simon Rich isn't interested in condemning religion—he just wants to have fun with it, using the Bible as an outrageous vehicle with which to present, in his own odd way, questions about faith and human nature.... Rich knows how to balance the smart with the funny."
—Patrick Cassels, *New York Times Book Review*

"A divine satire."—Alfred Hickling, *The Guardian* (UK)

"Sweetly funny and even moving; love, in this case, is what makes the world keep spinning."

—Kate Tuttle, *Boston Globe*

"This depiction of the Almighty as an affable-but-oblivious overgrown frat boy probably isn't what you'd expect, especially if you happen to belong to a religion in which God does not use profanity and refer to 'Free Bird' as his 'jam.' But that's the beauty of *Miracle Workers*, the fourth book from *Saturday Night Live* writer Rich—it's as unpredictable as it is funny, and it's one of the best American comic novels of the past few years.... Not too many authors could pull off a plot this gleefully absurd.... Comedy that mocks and insults people is the easiest thing in the world to do, but it's infinitely harder to be both funny and kind. Rich displays a real love for his characters.... The young author has an obvious affection for the underdog, and a soft spot for those who work hard at what they do. It's that sensibility that makes *Miracle Workers* a near-perfect work of humor writing—strikingly original, edgy but compassionate, and, most importantly, deeply hilarious."

—Michael Schaub, National Public Radio

"Simon Rich, one of the funniest writers in America, creates a God that's Old Testamenty.... Rich evokes enough of the hellish qualities of Earth (Lynyrd Skynyrd, Walmart, a screenplay for *Finnegans Wake*) and of the little things that we'll miss (Lynyrd Skynyrd, Walmart, a screenplay for *Finnegans Wake*) that it feels like a little love letter to the world. Thanks, life. Good of you to let me drop by." —Jimmy So, *Daily Beast*

"Rich's play on office politics and his understanding of the comic potential of human relationships is accurate enough, producing an appealing mixture of subtle and laugh-out-loud funny."

—Lesley McDowell, *The Independent* (UK)

"Rich's prose is admirably crisp and clear."

—Morley Walker, *Winnipeg Free Press*

"A brief, witty romp."

—Sheerly Avni, *Jewish Daily Forward*

"The author has the difficult task of sustaining the superb comic premise throughout a book-length work, which he accomplishes by having his outlandishly capricious God appear at regular intervals. Deliciously funny." —*Kirkus Reviews*

Also by Simon Rich

Elliot Allagash

Free-Range Chickens

Ant Farm: And Other Desperate Situations

Man Seeking Woman

The Married Kama Sutra (with Farley Katz)

Spoiled Brats

Hits and Misses

Miracle Workers

A Novel

Simon Rich

BACK BAY BOOKS
Little, Brown and Company
NEW YORK BOSTON LONDON

The characters and events in this book are fictitious. Any similarity to real persons, living or dead, is coincidental and not intended by the author.

Back Bay Books / Little, Brown and Company
Hachette Book Group
1290 Avenue of the Americas, New York, NY 10104
littlebrown.com

Originally published in hardcover by Little, Brown and Company, August 2012
First Back Bay trade paperback edition, August 2013
First Back Bay media tie-in paperback edition, January 2019

Back Bay Books is an imprint of Little, Brown and Company, a division of Hachette Book Group, Inc. The Back Bay Books name and logo are trademarks of Hachette Book Group, Inc.

Previously published as *What in God's Name*

ISBN 978-0-316-13373-9 (hc) / 978-0-316-25055-9 (lp) /
978-0-316-13374-6 (pb) / 978-0-316-48636-1 (mti pb)
LCCN 2012011106

10 9 8 7 6 5 4 3 2 1

LSC-C

Printed in the United States of America

For Nat, my idol

So God created man in his own image...

—*Genesis 1:27*

Part I

THE CEO LEANED BACK IN his swivel chair and flicked on his flat-screen TV. There was some kind of war going on in Venezuela. He forced himself to watch for a few minutes—it was the type of thing that people would expect him to know about. Last week at a meeting, some woman had asked him if he'd "heard about Ghana." He'd grinned and given her a thumbs-up because he knew Ghana had just qualified for the World Cup. But it turned out she'd been talking about a genocide.

He squinted hard at the TV, but within a few minutes, his eyes were glazed over with boredom. He decided to take a quick break. He would watch something else for five minutes, ten minutes max. Then he would flip back to the Venezuela thing.

He pressed the "favorite" button on his remote control and an overweight man appeared on the screen. He had three huge splotches of sweat on his shirt, two under his armpits and one in the center of his stomach.

"Let me hear it!" the man was shouting into a microphone. "Let me hear it for the *glory of God!*"

The CEO flipped to another church channel and then another. Sometimes when he got going with the church channels, he couldn't stop himself. He loved the forceful cadence of the ministers—the way the people shook and moaned with spirit.

He flipped to a Baptist service in Memphis. An elderly woman was sprinting back and forth across a stage, slapping her face and body like she was trying to escape from killer bees.

"Praise God!" she was screaming. "Praise *God,* praise *God,* praise..."

A young man poked his head into the office.

"God? Are you busy?"

God quickly flipped back to the war.

"Um...just trying to do something about this Venezuela thing!" he said, gesturing vaguely at the TV. "There's a war there."

"Oh!" the young Angel said. "I didn't mean to interrupt!"

"No biggie. What can I do for you?"

"It's time for your ten o'clock meeting?"

God looked at his watch and chuckled.

"How about that?" he said. "Must've lost track of time!"

The Angel led God down the hallway toward the executive boardroom. He thought about making small talk, but he couldn't think of anything to say. The truth was, he was still pretty intimidated by his boss. Craig had worked at Heaven Inc. for five years, but this was actually the first time he'd spoken to God in person.

The opportunity had come about totally by chance. He was drinking some coffee when one of the Archangels smacked him on the back and said, "Hey, Page, bring God to the boardroom."

Craig was an Angel, a full two rungs higher than a Page, but he hadn't bothered to correct him; he knew from experience that there was no point in reasoning with an Archangel. Besides, he was grateful for the chance to finally see God's office.

It had fulfilled all of his expectations. God's TV was enormous—at least sixty inches—and his remote control was *nuts*—a shiny, chrome slab that looked like it had been molded to fit his hand. The desk was solid maple and covered with cool executive toys. There was a Rubik's Cube (which Craig could see was impressively far along) and a gleaming executive ball clicker, the kind that swings for minutes on end when given the slightest push.

Craig located the boardroom and, with some difficulty,

pulled open the heavy brass door. God strolled in and Craig tried to follow, but a strong hand clamped down on his shoulder. It was Vince, a gigantically tall Archangel with slick blond hair.

"Sorry," he said, grinning down at him. "Management only."

On his way back down to the lowly Miracles Department, Craig tried to imagine what was happening behind that boardroom door. They were making huge decisions up there—massive, cataclysmic pronouncements that would affect the fates of billions. He would do anything, he thought, just to sit at that table.

Vince unscrewed his fountain pen.

"NFL?" he asked.

God closed his eyes and massaged his temples.

"Packers," he said finally.

The Archangels murmured their approval. Vince wrote down "Packers" on a legal pad and circled it.

"We'll make it happen," he assured him. "What about NASCAR?"

"I like Trevor Bayne," God said. "And David Reutimann."

Vince wrote down the drivers' names.

"NHL?"

God shrugged. "No preference."

He pointed suddenly at Vince. "Hey, how are my numbers?"

Vince swiftly removed a pie graph from his briefcase.

"Your numbers are *fantastic,*" he said. "Eighty-five percent of humans worship you in some way."

"Outstanding," God said, smiling proudly at the chart. "Any problem demographics?"

Vince hesitated. "Some college kids have doubts," he admitted. "But we think they'll come around."

"You sure?"

The Archangel nodded vigorously. "It's just a phase."

God squinted at him. "What about Lynyrd Skynyrd?" he asked. "Whatever happened with that?"

Vince swallowed. Lynyrd Skynyrd was God's favorite band, and for months he'd been pressuring his Archangels to somehow reunite the original lineup.

"I'm not sure it's feasible," Vince said. "I mean... half of the founding members are dead."

"What about the guys who are left? Gary Rossington? Larry Junstrom? If you got those guys together in a room, I bet they could still rock."

Vince sighed. "We'll keep working on it."

God folded his arms. "And the Yankees?"

"Up three games," Vince said, quickly pulling another chart out of his briefcase. "And A-Rod's got a twenty-game hit streak."

God leaned back in his chair and smiled.

"All right, then," he said. "Let's play golf!"

* * *

Craig returned to the main floor of the Miracles Department, a grid of tiny cubicles where he spent the vast majority of his life. The place looked even gloomier than usual, now that he had seen God's office and the palatial boardroom where the Archangels did business. But as soon as he sat down at his desk and turned on his computer, his bitterness faded. On the screen, flashing brightly, was a Potential Miracle. He clicked on the link, and the computer zoomed in on a tiny street in Mobile, Alabama. A boy and girl were walking home from summer school, looking bored and miserable in the brutal August heat. Craig waited patiently as they approached a nearby fire hydrant. Then he spiked the subterranean pressure and made the hydrant erupt, drenching the kids with a burst of ice-cold water. They danced under the deluge, shrieking with laughter.

Craig couldn't believe it. His trip upstairs had distracted him so much he'd almost missed a hydrant miracle. He felt so guilty—he should never have left his desk.

He scanned the globe and quickly found another Potential Miracle. A middle-aged woman in New Brunswick was wearing an old jacket and had no idea her pockets were filled with cash. Craig hit her with a harsh gust of wind, and after muttering a few intense curse words, she shoved her hands inside her coat for warmth. Within seconds she was pumping her fist in the air, a wad of crumpled twenties in her hand.

Craig leaned back and smiled. The woman was dancing in the empty parking lot now, slapping her buttocks aggressively in a kind of improvised Macarena. There was nothing more exhilarating than watching humans celebrate your miracles. Craig allowed himself to watch for thirty seconds, then closed the window. If he let himself get sidetracked, he would never get anything done. It was time to move on to the next one.

A tourist in Monte Carlo was walking toward an obviously rigged roulette table. Craig was trying to divert the poor guy's path when a knock interrupted his thought process.

"Craig?"

A lanky young woman with oversized glasses was peering into his cubicle.

"Sorry for interrupting," she said, sticking out her hand. "I'm Eliza."

"Oh *no!* I totally forgot you were coming. Have you been waiting long?"

"Since nine," she said, smiling brightly to conceal her annoyance.

"I'm so sorry. How can I make it up to you?"

"Well, I'd love a tour. If you're not busy."

Craig glanced at his computer screen. The tourist had taken a seat at the roulette table and placed an enormous sum on black. It was too late to fix things.

"No problem," Craig said. "Follow me!"

* * *

Eliza had just been promoted to the Miracles Department after toiling for three long years as a Sub-Angel in Prayer Intake. Craig had agreed to show her around her new floor, but his trip upstairs had seriously delayed him. Eliza had spent her first morning as an Angel in the break room, checking her BlackBerry over and over in search of an explanation. She was furious that Craig had made her wait so long, but her anger quickly subsided in the excitement of the tour.

She eagerly swiveled her head around as Craig walked her through the bustling office. Everywhere she looked, Angels were scanning the globe, typing in codes, changing the world with a few little taps of their fingers. It was as wonderful as she'd imagined.

"Fuck!" someone shouted.

Eliza glanced into a nearby cubicle. An older, balding Angel had spilled his coffee, and the murky brown liquid was seeping across his keyboard. He pulled some random papers out of his inbox and used them to sponge up the mess.

"Every time," he muttered. "Every fucking time."

"Who's that?" Eliza whispered.

"That's Brian," Craig told her. "He's going through a rough time."

"Do you guys work together?"

"Nah, we're in different subdepartments. I'm General Well-Being, he's Physical Safety."

"So he prevents accidents?"

"Well... he tries to."

Eliza peeked into Brian's cubicle. His computer monitor was divided into sixteen windows, each one depicting a different Potential Injury. The injuries ranged in seriousness from stubbed toes to first-degree burns, but they all had one thing in common: they were preventable. Eliza watched as the victims yelled out profanities on Brian's screen. Some of the humans directed their swearing heavenward, as if they somehow knew that Brian was responsible for their pain.

"Goddammit," said an old woman, who had just sliced open her thumb on a tuna fish can. *"Motherfucker."*

Brian closed his eyes and rubbed his face, taking deep, slow breaths.

"How does he stop the injuries?" Eliza asked. "Or, you know... try to."

"It's the same as any miracle," Craig explained. "Angelic Influence."

He led her to a nearby closet and handed her a thick leather-bound book. She flipped through the pages, squinting at the dense charts.

"I know it looks confusing," Craig sympathized. "But after a while all this stuff becomes second nature."

Eliza pointed at a foldout table labeled Gusts. "What's this one?"

"That comes in handy if you need to move something. Like if you need to get a beach towel out of the way so a human can find his car keys."

Eliza unfolded the Gusts chart. It was forty pages long, plus footnotes.

"Why can't we just zap the keys into the guy's pocket?"

Craig laughed. "I know, right? It would make things way easier. Unfortunately, though, we can't break any laws."

"Which laws?"

"*God's* laws. Gravity, thermodynamics, time. They're ironclad. We have to work around them."

"So we can't, like, resurrect people. Or make them fly."

"Right. There's no teleporting, no telepathy, no making objects disappear. We can't do anything that the humans could perceive as supernatural."

"So we can't do anything fun."

Craig grinned. "I don't know about that."

EARTH

Oscar Friedman opened his *Boston Herald* and held it in front of his face like a shield. He just had to make it through three more stops without being seen. Just five more minutes and he'd be home free.

"Are you sure it's your old roommate?" his wife whispered.

Oscar nodded. It was definitely him, sitting across from them on the inbound Red Line. And he had definitely forgotten the man's name.

"I know it starts with an R," Oscar murmured.

"Is it Rick? Richard?"

Oscar shook his head and motioned frantically to his wife for more suggestions.

"Ronny? Reginald?"

Oscar clenched his eyes shut. "I've almost got it," he said. "I'm so damn close."

"Ross? Red?"

It was too late. The roommate had already made eye contact and was lurching gaily across the car. He weaved his way around a pole and gripped Oscar's elbow with both hands.

"Oscar, it's been forever! We missed you at the reunion."

Oscar shot his wife a terrified look, and she quickly thrust out her hand.

"I'm Florence," she tried.

The roommate ignored her and playfully folded his arms.

"What's the matter, Oscar? Aren't you going to introduce me to your lovely wife?"

Oscar was about to confess the truth when the lights flickered out. The blackout lasted forty seconds, precisely long enough to jog his memory. And by the time the bulbs flashed back on, and the conductor stopped barking over the loudspeaker, the old man was beaming with relief.

"Honey," he said, "this is *Roland!*"

"We can only affect the lives of humans *indirectly,*" Craig explained. "Through discreet use of natural phenomena. We can cause electrical blackouts, make hail, use lightning. We can control the tides and trigger sneezes. We just can't do anything that would let the humans know we're here."

"Does anyone ever screw up?" Eliza asked. "You know, cross the line?"

Craig thought it over. Angels rarely got punished for their miracles. But he could think of a couple of instances where one of them had gone too far, gotten too flashy, and ended up out of a job.

"Someone got in trouble for Wilt Chamberlain," he said.

"Really? What happened?"

Craig told her the story. It was 1962, and a first-year Angel had been assigned to a regular season matchup between the New York Knicks and the Philadelphia Warriors. The Angel was supposed to support Wilt Chamberlain—God was a fan—but he went way too far. Wilt, normally a 50 percent foul shooter, hit twenty-eight out of thirty-two free throws that night and ended up scoring one hundred points. It was one of the sloppiest miracles in the history of sports. Not only was the number too high, it was cartoonish.

"If Wilt had scored ninety-seven points," Craig explained. "Or a hundred and three. That would be one thing. But *exactly* one hundred? It was too conspicuous. The Angel got demoted."

"That's awful."

Craig nodded. "It's best to fly under the radar. You can do as many miracles as you want—you just have to be subtle about them."

"What about God? Can his miracles break the rules?"

"Oh, God doesn't code any miracles himself."

"He doesn't?"

"Nah. That stuff is *really* technical. And he's really more of an ideas guy, you know? Ever since the beginning, he's hired people to take care of the nitty-gritty things for him. I don't think he's *ever* been involved in the company's day-to-day activities."

"Doesn't he care how things are going?"

"Oh, he cares!" Craig said. "This morning, I went to his office and he was monitoring the war situation in Venezuela."

Eliza spun around. "You were in his *office?* Why?"

Craig swallowed, noticing her sparkling blue eyes for the first time.

"Oh, you know," he said, "we just...we have that kind of relationship."

Craig led Eliza back to his computer and played her some of his recent miracles. A seventh-grader at a science fair smiled with relief as his shoddy clay volcano managed somehow to erupt. A truck driver turned right to avoid a fallen tree—and happened upon a stranded motorist.

"We manufacture coincidences," Craig explained. "The humans don't perceive them as miracles—but they *are.*"

Eliza beamed at him. "So it's *true,*" she said. "There *are* no coincidences—everything happens for a reason!"

Craig hesitated, reluctant to disillusion her.

"Actually," he admitted, "the truth is...ninety-nine percent of the things that happen to humans are just crazy and random and serve no function whatsoever."

"Oh."

He was worried he'd upset her, but her smile quickly returned.

"But the other one percent? Those are miracles, huh?"

Craig nodded.

"Well, hey!" she said. "That's something!"

Craig was thrilled to discover that Eliza had been assigned to the cubicle next to him. It would help her productivity, after all, to have a more experienced employee watching over her.

Eliza put her bag down on her new desk, then stood on top of her chair to have a look around. She grabbed Craig's arm for support, and his body shyly stiffened.

"What are they working on next door?" she asked.

Craig peered over the cubicle wall. Three exhausted Angels were huddled over a single computer, frantically typing in codes.

"Oh, they're on Lynyrd Skynyrd duty," Craig said. "Special orders from the man upstairs."

On the monitor two original members of Lynyrd Skynyrd were having a "coincidental" encounter at a gas station.

"What are the odds both our trucks would break down on the same road?"

"Pretty crazy."

"Hey... maybe we should jam again sometime?"

The three Angels sighed with relief. One of them opened a filing cabinet, took out a bottle of bourbon, and started drinking from it.

Eliza climbed back down.

"Are all the miracles assigned?" she asked, her voice tinged with disappointment.

"Actually," Craig said, "for the most part, we can do whatever we want! That's the great thing about working in this department. We're so low on the totem pole, nobody's really watching us."

A beeping noise sounded on Eliza's computer and she gave a startled hop.

"Don't worry," Craig said, "it's just a Potential Miracle."

She peered at her screen; a hungry Chinese teenager was kicking a vending machine in frustration, trying to dislodge the candy bar he'd just purchased.

"Why did *this* one come up?" Eliza asked.

"Oh, it's random. Our algorithms anticipate millions of PMs a second. That's way too much for us to handle, so the computer feeds them to us one at a time."

Eliza watched as the Chinese teenager hopped on his bicycle and glumly pedaled away from the vending machine.

"Oh no," she said. "I blew it."

Craig laughed. "Don't worry. You'll have plenty of chances. Click refresh."

She tapped her mouse, and the earth popped onto her screen, a glowing blue ball, as shiny as a Christmas ornament.

"Good luck," he said. "It's all yours."

Eliza swiveled around in her desk chair, marveling at the size of her new cubicle. When she was in Prayer Intake she'd had to beg her supervisors for a desk, and the one they finally gave her was in the hallway next to the bathrooms. It was a terrible place to work: noisy and smelly and lonely. Luckily, she was usually too busy to notice.

When Eliza first arrived in Prayer Intake, the department was in shambles. The prayers came in by fax—

usually about 500 million a day—and they were all heaped into the same gigantic storage room. Each night someone would fill a sack with random prayers and send it upstairs to God. The rest would end up in the incinerator. Eliza was appalled. Even though she was just a Sub-Angel, she immediately took it upon herself to change things.

After innumerable meetings, she was eventually able to implement a commonsense accounting system. Her first improvement was to staple identical prayers together, to save God time. The less God had to read, she reasoned, the more prayers he could answer. Next, she instituted a field-goal filter. A full 4 percent of prayers were related to field-goal attempts—and since an equal number of humans usually rooted for success or failure, she figured that none were worth answering.

But Eliza's crowning achievement was the Urgency Scale. For as long as anyone could remember, prayers had been sent upstairs at random. It didn't matter whether you asked for a new bike or a new kidney; they all had the same chance of reaching God's desk. On Eliza's watch, prayers were finally sorted by importance, on an easy-to-follow 1-to-7 ranking system.

About 30 percent of prayers were classified as 1s—meaning their urgency was low. Traffic prayers usually went into this category, along with lotto prayers, in-flight turbulence prayers, and prayers for wireless Internet access. Most prayers were classified as 3s or 4s:

parents wishing for the general health of their children, lovers hoping to see each other soon, abstract pleas for peace. Only matters of life and death were 7s. Under Eliza's watch, these were reprinted on special red stationery so they would stand out in God's inbox.

Her supervisor had fought her system because of all the extra work it would entail. And in order to get it approved, she'd had to promise to do all of the prayer sorting herself. It was tedious, even with the help of computers. She worked so many weekends, the word "Friday" lost all meaning. Every day was the same, a grueling endurance test that ended only when she reached her physical breaking point. But Eliza had persevered, driven by the knowledge that she was making a concrete difference in people's lives.

Of course, her motives weren't entirely selfless: she also wanted a promotion. Ever since she'd joined Heaven Inc., Eliza had dreamt of making it to the Miracles Department. When she was a Page, she used to volunteer to stock the vending machines on the seventeenth floor, just so she could catch a glimpse of the Angels in action. It was the most exciting, creative unit in the entire company. Sorting prayers was one thing—but planning miracles! What could possibly be cooler than that?

When she applied for a spot in the Miracles Department, her supervisor made fun of her for a solid hour. No Sub-Angel had ever jumped from Prayer Intake to

Miracles before—not in the department's entire history. He agreed to forward her résumé to Angel Resources, but only after reading the whole thing out loud, in a mock British accent, to a pack of laughing secretaries.

When Eliza received her congratulatory e-mail, she thought at first that her supervisor had sent it as a cruel practical joke. But the shock on his face when she told him the news convinced her the promotion was for real. He demanded to read the e-mail himself, and when she forwarded him the message he stared at it for a solid ten minutes. Eventually, he stiffly shook her hand and sent out a secretary to buy a bad bottle of champagne. Eliza forced down a glass, packed her stapler in a cardboard box, and wobbled trancelike to the elevators.

And now here she was, on the seventeenth floor, just a few strides away from the vending machine she had once begged permission to stock.

She knew it was irrational, but she kept expecting a second e-mail to arrive in her inbox—a short, apologetic note from Angel Resources—telling her there'd been a mistake. Any second now, she thought, someone—an embarrassed-looking man in a gray flannel suit, maybe—was going to knock on her cubicle and inform her as politely as he could that she would have to go back downstairs.

"There's no easy way to say this," he would begin. "But..."

She pictured herself returning to the fourth floor, tearfully unpacking her stapler while the secretaries stifled their giggles.

Eliza opened her new filing cabinet and spotted a small white envelope. She assumed it had been left there by the cubicle's previous occupant. But when she flipped it over, she saw with surprise that it had her name on it. She carefully opened the envelope and plucked out a shiny, wing-shaped pin. As she brought it toward her face, its silver coating glinted in the light.

She'd seen Angels wearing these pins around the commissary, and they'd always struck her as a bit silly. Why did they have to make them so garish? Wouldn't identification cards be more cost-effective? Still, she supposed she'd better put hers on. She'd noticed earlier that Craig was wearing one, so it was probably company policy.

She fastened the wings to her lapel and straightened them in the reflection of her computer monitor. "Eliza Hunter," the pin read in gold letters. "Angel: Miracles Dept."

She poked her head through the cubicle doorway to make sure no one was coming. Then she leaned back inside, closed her eyes, and thrust both arms into the air.

Craig shuffled down the hall, struggling to balance two large plates of cake. It was someone's birthday—he wasn't sure whose—and he had snatched the last two slices in the break room. He was just a few paces from his cubicle when he lost his footing and spilled one of the slices onto the floor. He cursed under his breath, scraped the mess off the carpet, and tossed it into a garbage can.

Craig looked at the remaining slice. It was a corner piece, thickly frosted on three sides. He hesitated for a moment, then knocked on Eliza's cubicle and handed it to her.

"Hey!" he said. "There was one slice left!"

"Wow, thanks. Sure you don't want it?"

"Nah," Craig said, unconvincingly. "Nah."

"Really?"

"Yeah," Craig said, holding his hands up in protest. "I'm actually, uh... allergic to chocolate."

Eliza blushed. In the past three days she'd seen Craig eat two Almond Joys and a twelve-pack of Oreos.

"Well, thanks, Craig."

"Sure! I mean... it's nothing."

He trudged back to his cubicle and slumped wearily into his chair. Allergic to chocolate? What the hell kind of lie was that? He shook his head, shocked by his stupidity. He could have just said he wasn't hungry. Or that he wanted her to have it.

He turned on his computer, determined to push the incident out of his mind. He'd already more or less clinched his second straight Angel of the Month award (his closest competition was twenty-two miracles behind). But if he allowed himself to get distracted, someone else could leap ahead of him. And that would be unacceptable, especially after all the sacrifices he'd made. He'd been coming to work on weekends and eating every meal at his desk. He'd even made a policy of avoiding dates and parties because they interfered with his late-night work schedule. Craig didn't have much of a social life, so this policy had never technically been tested. Still, it was a policy, and he was proud of it.

He scanned the globe for Potential Miracles, but he was having trouble concentrating. A nagging thought kept running through his mind, ruining his focus. Finally he stood up and poked his head over into Eliza's cubicle.

"There's milk," he said.

Eliza jumped. "What?"

"For your cake," Craig said. "In the fridge in the break room... there's milk there."

"Oh," she said. "Okay."

He spotted her plate in the trash can; she'd finished her slice a while ago. How much time had passed?

"Well, thanks," she said. "Now I know where the milk is."

"No problemo!" he said, using that phrase for the first time in his life.

He wasn't sure how to end the conversation, so he made a baffling hand gesture—a kind of half-wave, half-salute with vague hip-hop undertones. Then he sighed audibly and slowly slunk out of her view.

He stared at his reflection in his computer monitor; his cheeks were flushed and his forehead was damp with sweat. He felt ashamed and depressed—but also a little relieved. Now that he had ruined things, there was nothing to distract him; now he could finally get back to work.

"Hey, can you explain dreams again?"

"Sure. Milk or sugar?"

"Both."

Craig handed Eliza her coffee. The break room was empty and the department completely silent, except for the whir of a janitor's vacuum cleaner.

"Dreams were invented by Angels to test out their beta programs."

Eliza paused, embarrassed to be asking another question so quickly into the explanation.

"I'm sorry... what are beta programs again?"

"Oh, they're awesome. They're unreleased pieces of software. In dreams you can try out anything you want. You can break all the rules, consequence free."

"Which rules?"

"Well a lot of Angels really hate the gravity thing, so you see a bunch of flying programs. What else... a lot of teleporting and body morphing and resurrecting the dead."

Eliza added some more sugar to her coffee.

"Don't those dreams screw humans up?"

Craig shook his head. "They're self-erasing. As soon as you wake up, you forget almost everything that happened."

"Is that sort of like...?"

Craig nodded. "It's sort of like what happens when you die. You remember a couple things—a face or two, maybe, or a place. Then it fades."

She stirred her coffee and took a sip.

"Sometimes I think I remember something," she said. "Someone calling my name. I think it was Susan, maybe? Or Sarah? I don't know."

"The only thing I can remember," Craig said, "is working right here."

Eliza nodded. She could recall orientation so vividly: the endless PowerPoint presentations, the idiotic trust falls, the '80s-themed mixer. But everything before that was a blur.

"What's your favorite beta program?" she asked.

Craig bit into his Hostess cupcake.

"It'd have to be Vision Stuffer," he said. "That's the one that allows you to visit them. You know, to try to reason with them."

"Does that ever work?"

Craig laughed. "Nah. They usually forget what you told them by morning. And if anything sticks—like an image or a word—they fill in the blanks themselves and write a crazy book about you."

"So all of those religions..."

Craig nodded. "They're our fault."

He broke his second cupcake in half and slid a piece over to Eliza. She shook her head politely, but within a few seconds she was eating it.

"Thanks," she said. "I forgot to eat dinner."

"Me too. That's why I picked strawberry—it seemed like the healthiest cupcake flavor."

Eliza raised her eyebrows teasingly. "Plus you're allergic to chocolate."

Craig averted his eyes. "What were we talking about?"

Eliza smiled. "Heaven stuff."

"Right!" Craig said, relieved to be back on the subject of work. "Do you have any other questions?"

"Just one. How does he decide? You know, on who gets in?"

"I don't know," Craig admitted. "I've always wanted to ask him. But I've never had the guts."

"I'd love to know."

"Yeah. Me too."

She yawned suddenly, clasping her hands high above her head. Craig tried not to stare as her shirt climbed slowly up her midriff, revealing a sliver of her stomach. She almost definitely had a boyfriend. Some executive probably, with tailored suits and monogrammed ties. His name was probably James or Charles or...

"Craig?"

"What?"

"You were staring off into space."

"Oh—sorry. Just tired."

She leaned in slightly. "Thanks for showing me the ropes. I really appreciate it."

"Sure!" Craig said. "I mean, it's my job."

She finished her coffee in a single swallow and left him alone in the break room.

Craig's breath was shallow, and his heart was racing—but when he returned to his cubicle and turned on his computer, a sense of calm enveloped him. A thirty-four-year-old in Amsterdam needed to bike through traffic in time to feed his daughter's gerbil. This he understood—this he could handle.

In the last three years Craig had gone on exactly one date. He didn't have much of a frame of reference, but he could tell the encounter had gone poorly. His first mistake, he realized in hindsight, was to insist that the girl meet him in the office cafeteria. He was just a Sub-Angel back then, in Snowflake Design, and he'd been too anxious to leave his cubicle for more than thirty minutes at a time.

He couldn't decide whether or not the girl was pretty, in part because he was too shy to look directly at her. But she seemed like a nice person, and the following week he worked up the courage to call her again.

"I don't think it's a good idea," she said. "You're just too work-obsessed for me."

"What?" Craig asked. He was designing a snowflake at the time and wasn't fully listening to her.

"You're too *work-obsessed*," she repeated.

"Oh," he said.

Craig knew his obsession with work was unusual, but he couldn't control it. His job was his entire identity. Craig, like all his coworkers, lived on the Heaven Campus, a sprawling enclave of dormitories, office buildings, and snack bars. His home was only five minutes away from his office—less if he scootered to work. It was convenient but also vaguely depressing. Heaven was so vast, yet his entire life took place within a single square acre of it.

Craig didn't have to be an Angel. Most people in heaven were content to work as Pages or secretaries, sleepwalking through their term of service until it was time to retire. God required forty years of work, but it didn't matter which job you picked. Most Heaven Inc. employees spent less than five hours a day in the office. The campus had everything: tennis courts, bocce, a koi pond. It was crazy to spend all your time indoors.

But whenever Craig signed up for a golf lesson or rented a rowboat, he felt ridiculous. There were a lot of fun things to do in heaven. But none were as thrilling as what you could do on Earth.

There were so many things in Craig's life that he

couldn't control: his carpal tunnel symptoms, his mounting insomnia, his nonexistent social life. But he could control the humans. He could grant them small victories, divert their little tragedies, deliver them some tiny measures of happiness. He knew it was madness to spend so much time obsessing over them. They had no idea he even existed. His miracles were invisible by design—and always would be. Still, on some level, he felt like the species was counting on him. And he didn't want to let them down.

Sometimes, when he needed cheering up, he watched clips of children celebrating all the snow days he had caused. One girl, an eighth-grade outcast from Sweden, was so thrilled when she heard that school was canceled that she immediately started break-dancing. Her moves were so infectious that Craig stood up in his cubicle and danced along with her, shaking his hips and pumping his fists in the air. It was the happiest moment of his career.

He knew his miracles were small and often ridiculous. But he loved every single one of them. It was only when he turned off his computer and took the lonely elevator ride down that he sometimes wondered: Did the humans really need him? Or was it the other way around?

Eliza watched as the night janitor put on his coat and lumbered out of the office. It was seven in the morning. She'd spent all night on a father-son fishing trip in

Arkansas, trying in vain to hook them some bass. She'd scrutinized the chapter on Current Manipulation, but most of it had gone right over her head.

How did Craig make the job look so easy? She knew it was inappropriate, but she'd peeked at his computer after he'd gone home. He'd already completed several miracles this week, and all of them were pretty cool.

In Portugal he broke a Ben and Jerry's freezer, compelling the manager to give away his melting ice cream for free.

In Melbourne he rigged an old man's iPod to play the Beatles' song "Birthday" over and over again until he remembered to buy his wife a gift.

In Oxford he anticipated that an elderly professor was about to refer to his only black student, Charles, as "Jamal." He quickly short-circuited the fire alarm, emptying the classroom just in time.

He loosened a piñata for a puny third-grader in Puebla, shocking the boy's peers and transforming him into a cult hero.

He made thirteen shooting stars, eleven rainbows, and a hundred and forty breezes.

And she couldn't even hook a single fish.

She squinted at her pasty reflection in the computer monitor. She had to pace herself. She was less than a week into the job, and she already resembled that pathetic cliché—the scraggly, burnt-out Angel. She leaned back in her chair, and her spine cracked audibly, a series of disturbing pops. She would give the miracle one more try and then she'd give up on it.

"Come on, you stupid fish..."

She paused. Something was wrong.

"What the fuck?"

Her computer started to beep as a line of text flashed nightmarishly on the screen.

Unnatural Currents Detected.
Code Black.

She checked Craig's cubicle, but he hadn't shown up yet. No one had; she was the only person on the floor. She rummaged through her desk, knocking over several half-filled coffee cups before she found the manual. It was an enormous book, the size of a hatbox, with tiny type and pages so thin they were translucent.

"Code Black, Code Black..."

It took her five minutes to find it and another ten to accept the reality of the situation.

Code Black: Possible tsunami.
Potential loss of life.
Warn God.

She scanned the office one more time, but it was still completely empty. She thought about waiting for Craig to arrive, but the code kept flashing insistently, the beeping getting faster with every passing second.

Eventually, she stood up and sprinted toward the elevators.

"You can't see him right now," Vince said, kicking his feet onto his desk. "He's busy."

"But I have a Code Black. A possible tsunami!"

"You can make an appointment," Vince suggested. "But there's a two-month wait."

"I can't wait two months!"

"I don't know what to tell you, honey."

Eliza's vision was blurry from exhaustion, but she thought she could detect a smirk on the Archangel's face.

"Fuck this," she muttered.

Vince laughed incredulously as Eliza shoved open the brass door.

"Page! Where are you going?"

"I'm an Angel," she corrected. "And I'm going to talk to God."

God liked eggs in the morning. It didn't really matter which kind. Poached, fried, scrambled. Sometimes he had them bring him what he called a bird's nest: a piece of toast with an egg stuck in the middle.

He removed the silver dome with a flourish. Scrambled. Perfect.

God looked at his watch and smiled proudly. This was

the third morning in a row he'd gotten to work on time. If he did two more, he'd tie his record. He flipped on the television and switched it to NASCAR.

A reporter was interviewing Trevor Bayne about his recent winning streak.

"I just want to thank God," he was saying. "I wouldn't be where I am without him."

God shook his head and laughed. He loved that Bayne guy.

He was almost finished with his eggs when the race began. He grabbed the remote and cranked up the volume.

"Come on, Bayne," he said, shaking salt onto his eggs. *"Focus."*

There was a soft knock on his door. He'd asked for Tabasco. Maybe this was it?

"Come on in," he called out cheerfully.

A young woman he'd never seen before came into the room. She was very attractive, he noticed, but haggard-looking. Her bright blue eyes were barely visible beneath drooping lids. And her long, thin body was stooped like an old man's. God shook his head. He could never understand it when a pretty young woman worked hard.

"You bring the Tabasco?" he asked.

"Excuse me?"

"Tabasco?"

"No...uh...I'm here to tell you about a Code Black? The computer said I should warn you."

God nodded. Bayne's lead had shrunk by more than half. How had that happened?

"I'm sorry for interrupting," Eliza said. "But it said there was a potential loss of life."

God motioned for her to take a seat and turned up the volume on his television.

"You like racing?" he asked. "This is a big one—Bayne's going for his second straight win at Daytona."

Eliza nodded awkwardly. "If you're not too busy," she said, "I think you should take a look at the tsunami. It seems like a pretty urgent situation."

"Move, Bayne! Finish strong! I'm sorry, what?"

"It seems like an urgent situation."

God nodded. "You're right. I'll intervene."

Eliza exhaled with relief. "Thank you."

God opened his e-mail account and tapped out a message to Vince, typing with two outstretched index fingers. Then he leaned back in his chair, grabbed the remote, and turned up the television as loud as it would go.

"Bayne and Collins are neck and neck!" the announcer shouted. *"Collins is making a push…a big push! He's three lengths ahead…he should win this one easily and…oh, no! He's down! His car has flipped end over end! He's escaped the wreckage, but he's on fire…wow…he really seems to be in a lot of pain. Looks like Trevor Bayne is the winner. Although I'm sure he didn't want to win like this."*

God chuckled.

"Sir," Eliza said. "When you said you were going to intervene...were you talking about the car race or the tsunami?"

God made eye contact with her for the first time. "What tsunami?"

Something on the TV caught his eye. "Hey—they're interviewing Bayne!"

The racer lifted a trophy over his head and leaned toward a cluster of microphones. "I just want to thank God for this victory," he began. "I couldn't have done it without him."

God clapped his hands. "Did you hear that? Did you hear what he just said?"

Eliza forced a smile. "Yeah. Neat."

"Man...I *love* that Bayne guy."

God turned off the television.

"Okay," he said. "I'm sorry. Where's the earthquake?"

"It's a tsunami. And I'm not sure where it is—it just said 'possible.' It came in this morning, around seven?"

God stroked his chin. "Probably too late to stop it. I tell you what: I'll inform my prophet."

He turned the television back on and flipped to a new channel. A wiry man in rags stood by the side of a highway, holding a cardboard sign.

Eliza squinted incredulously at the screen. "That's your prophet?"

God nodded. "I'll tell him to warn the people with a sign. Something blunt, like 'The End Is Near.' "

Eliza stared at the screen. The filthy man waved at her.

"God," she whispered, "with all due respect... couldn't you have picked a better prophet?"

God shrugged. "What's wrong with Raoul?"

"I just feel like if you sent your messages through a scientist, say, or a president, more people would pay attention."

"I've been giving Raoul the straight dope since he was seventeen. If the humans don't want to listen to him, that's their problem."

The telephone rang and God scooped up the receiver.

"Yeah, three o'clock's good. Let's just play nine this time, though. My back's killing me."

Raoul winked at Eliza. "Hey, pretty lady," he said.

She turned away from the screen.

"Don't worry about the tsunami," God told her, holding his palm over the phone. "I've got everything taken care of."

Eliza nodded wearily and shuffled across the carpet. She was almost out the door when she spotted something odd. In the corner of God's office was a giant stack of papers, a towering column that was nearly as tall as she was. She squinted at the heap and noticed that the pages had a familiar red tint. It was a pile of prayers—all 7s.

Eliza suddenly felt dizzy. She slipped out the door, got into the elevator, and rode down to 17.

When the doors slid open, she cringed at the burst of fluorescent light. The floor was packed with Angels now, shouting into their BlackBerrys, pounding on their keyboards, chugging coffee from thermoses.

She went into her cubicle and noticed that her computer monitor was still flashing. The beeping had stopped, though.

Someone had turned off the sound.

"You went to God with a *code?*"

Craig clasped his scalp in disbelief. "What were you thinking?"

"I had to," Eliza said. "The whole thing was my fault."

She covered her face with her hands. "I was messing with currents," she said, her voice muffled by her fingers. "I screwed everything up."

"Don't worry!" Craig said. "Stuff like that happens *all the time*. In my first year, when I was trying to figure out wind currents, I caused over a dozen tornadoes."

Eliza spread her fingers a bit, peeking at Craig through the gap.

"Really?"

Craig nodded firmly. "Really."

"What did you do?" she asked.

"There was nothing I *could* do. I just pressed F7."

"Did that stop the tornadoes?"

Craig laughed. "No," he said. "It stopped the beeping."

Eliza's hands began to tremble slightly.

"Are you all right?" Craig asked.

She shook her head.

"I spent years sorting those prayers. And he didn't even read them. I mean, honestly, what kind of CEO is he? How incompetent can you get?"

Craig craned his neck around to make sure no one had witnessed her outburst.

"Look," he said. "I know he isn't much of a details guy. But you've got to give the man a little respect. I mean, this whole company was his idea. None of us would even be here without him. He deserves some credit."

"We have ten Angels working full-time on Lynyrd Skynyrd."

"Well, they're a great band." He ticked off their hits on his palm. "'Free Bird,' 'Sweet Home Alabama,' 'Simple Man'...those are all winners. Everyone can agree on those."

Eliza did not respond.

"At least he told his prophet," Craig offered. "That's something, right?"

"God's prophet is a naked homeless person! Every time he delivers a message, the humans think he's schizophrenic!"

"Well, that's not Raoul's fault. You can't put that on Raoul."

The blood drained from Eliza's face. "I feel sick," she murmured.

She bolted to the bathroom, and Craig leapt spryly out of the way. He was in a good mood. He'd just received an e-mail from Angel Resources informing him that he'd clinched another Angel of the Month award. The prize was pretty good this time: a coupon for a medium pizza of his choice. There was some fine print on the back of the coupon: deep-dish pies cost extra, he couldn't order more than three meat toppings, and the offer expired in fifteen days. Still, it was an excuse to ask Eliza to eat lunch with him.

He pictured them sitting together in the commissary, feasting on a pie topped with up to three meats.

"I can't believe you just *won* this," she'd say. "A whole pizza."

"There's more where that came from," he'd say. And things would progress from there somehow.

When she emerged from the bathroom, Craig hopped out of his chair, determined to make his move. But her grim expression gave him pause. She looked exhausted and worn out. The last thing he wanted was to annoy her when she was already feeling down.

Besides, it's not like he had anything that special to offer her. It was just a medium pizza, barely enough for two people. And what if she wanted more than three meats? It would be mortifying if his coupon was rejected.

"You know what?" Eliza told him. "I'm going to go back up there."

Craig squinted at her. "Did you forget something?"

She bit into her thumbnail, gnawed on it briefly, and then tore off a giant sliver. Craig winced as she plucked the half-moon shard from her tongue and flicked it onto the floor. Some of her nails were so mangled, he noticed, they had started to bleed.

"I'm going back up there," she said, "and I'm going to tell him to read those prayers. I spent three years sorting them. He doesn't have to answer them, but the least he can do is read them."

"Maybe you should go home? Get some sleep?"

"I'm not tired," she snapped, inserting a pinkie into her mouth.

Craig felt a sudden bizarre urge to grab her hand so that she would stop biting her fingernails.

"Wish me luck," she said.

There was nothing Craig could do. "Good luck," he said miserably.

God liked to drink beer out of a glass. He couldn't put his finger on why. It's not like the glass changed the way the beer tasted or made it any colder. There was just something classy about it, something dignified. It made you feel good about drinking beer, even if you were alone in your office and it was the middle of the workday.

He topped off his drink and turned on his flat-screen TV. It felt like a good time to check in with his prophet. He found him by the side of a highway in Detroit, waving a cardboard sign and wearing a suit made entirely of tinfoil.

"Hey, Raoul," God said. "How's it hanging?"

Raoul shrugged. "Low and lazy."

God laughed. "Cool outfit," he said. "Is it all foil?"

Raoul nodded. "It took six whole rolls. Everyone's been calling me crazy. But I think *they're* crazy."

God grinned. He loved Raoul's attitude, the way he let things roll right off his back. He was glad he'd picked him to be this century's prophet.

"So what's the word?" Raoul asked, taking out a fresh cardboard sign and a Sharpie.

"What do you mean?"

"What's your message? For me to tell the other humans?"

God looked down at his lap. He didn't actually *have* a message for the humans right now. But he didn't want to confess the truth—that he'd only phoned Raoul because he was lonely. He took a slow sip of beer, stalling.

"'The End Is Near,'" he said finally. "'Repent.'"

Raoul nodded. "I'll write it on my sign."

"Great!" God said. "That's great, Raoul. Take care."

He turned off the television and glanced at his watch. It was more than two hours until his afternoon meeting, and he had absolutely nothing to do. He picked up his Rubik's Cube and fooled around with it for a bit. He was almost finished with the yellow side, but he couldn't make any progress without messing up the red side. And he didn't want to do that—the red side was the only one he'd finished. After a few frustrating minutes, he twisted the cube back the way it had been and tossed it onto his desk.

God reclined listlessly in his chair. He couldn't admit it to anyone, but lately he'd been feeling pretty down on himself. His numbers had been slipping for years. Yes, over 80 percent of humans still believed in him. But in some East Coast cities, he barely had a majority. The Archangels told him it was nothing to worry about, that these things were "cyclical," but how could he trust them? They were just a bunch of slick-talking yes-men.

He knew it was unhealthy, but sometimes he looked himself up on the computer to see what people were saying about him. It was terrible for his self-esteem, but he couldn't stop himself. It was like trying not to scratch a scab; you could only fight the urge for so long. Sooner or later you had to see what was going on beneath the surface.

He turned on his computer, took a swig of beer, and typed his name into the search box: G...O...D.

Within seconds, he was watching a conversation in a dirty college dormitory.

"If there is a God," a girl human was saying, "like, sitting up there and watching all this on some cloud? Then he's an *asshole.*"

A boy human nodded and handed her some marijuana, as if her comment was so clever it deserved a reward.

God winced as the two humans laughed and then, inexplicably, began to make out. He knew they were young and immature and that he shouldn't put any stock in their opinions. But he couldn't help but feel hurt. An asshole? How could you say that about someone you'd never even met? The boy had oral herpes, and God thought about trying to spread it to the girl as a punishment. But he didn't want to make the humans suffer. He just wanted them to like him.

God double-clicked his mouse, closing the window. He wouldn't do any more searches for the rest of the day, he told himself. After this last one.

Someone was saying his name in Berlin, over and over again, with increasing volume. He clicked on the link with excitement—maybe it was one of those soapbox preachers, praising his name in front of a giant crowd!

God leaned forward, an expectant smile on his face. But his grin quickly faded when the window finished loading: it was a businessman who'd walked into a puddle and was taking his name in vain.

"Oh my fucking God," the man muttered, angrily shaking his foot out of a puddle. "What the fuck!"

God threw up his hands, exasperated. Why was this guy so mad at him? It's not like he had put the puddle there; puddles were just something that happened when it rained. Honestly, what was he supposed to do? He could say "No more rain," but that would probably cause even *more* problems for the humans and make them even angrier. He turned off the computer. Earth was just as frustrating as a Rubik's Cube. It was impossible to fix something without making another thing even worse. He reached for his beer mug and noticed with mild surprise that it was empty. He cracked open another can and took a giant swig, forgetting about the glass this time.

God knew that criticism was part of the job. You couldn't build something as successful as the world without hearing from some haters. But lately things had gotten out of hand. Recently one of the humans, Richard something, had written an entire book saying he didn't exist. God didn't mind at first; it was just some fancy-pants Oxford professor trying to get attention. But then the book had become an international bestseller. Now, it seemed like whenever he turned on human television, there the guy was, loudly holding forth on some talk show. God tried to read the book, but it hurt his feelings so much he had to stop after just a few pages. The blurb on the jacket said the author was a "fiery intellectual," but really he was just plain mean. God thought idly about having him killed or burning his face off, but that seemed like making too big a deal out of things.

God knew that his obsession with the humans was insane. When he first built the universe, after all, he'd never even intended for it to be populated. He'd constructed the earth for one reason and one reason only: to manufacture xenon gas. It was an extremely valuable element—rare, clean, potent—and the earth's atmosphere produced tons of it automatically. The Department of Xenon was the most important segment of God's company—it occupied seventy-four of the eighty-two floors of corporate headquarters. But God rapidly grew bored with that side of the business. The profits were so steady, it was a waste of time to even check the numbers. So one day, for amusement, he'd had his staff invent mankind. The humans had no effect on the production of xenon gas and therefore served no real function. But God quickly became preoccupied with the tiny creatures. Soon, to the dismay of his business managers, they were taking up almost all of his time. He began to care about their sports and their wars and their songs and their discoveries; most of all, he cared about what they thought of him. He created whole departments to maintain their planet and improve their lives. He recruited former humans to serve as Angels, erasing their memories and giving them new identities so they could focus on helping mankind. There was just something about those humans; they reminded God of himself.

God thought wistfully about the past. In the beginning, the humans were so easy to please. Give them some fruit, some light, and they'd all be singing his praises. Life expectancy was thirty years, and everybody was cool with that. If you started to go bald, you didn't curse God, you threw him a feast of thanks for allowing you to live so long.

These days nobody said thank you. God enjoyed all of the churches, especially the weirdo ones in the South. But it had been 5,127 years since anyone had offered him a proper ritual blood sacrifice. He never complained about it, because he didn't want to be "that guy." But it was definitely something that kept him up at night. It made him wonder if his best days were behind him; it made him wonder if it was time to retire.

He picked up his Rubik's Cube and rotated it a few times in his palm. There was probably a way to fix things, to set the world right. But he was too exhausted to figure it out. He squinted at the cube, with its jumbled splotches of blue and green. And then, with a shrug, he tossed it into the garbage.

"I'm sorry," Vince told God. "I told her you were busy."

God put down his golf clubs. That strange girl was back, the tired one who'd forgotten his Tabasco.

"So you're just going to play golf," Eliza said, her voice raspy from fatigue. "You're just going to ditch the office and hit the course."

God nodded, confused. "Do you...want to come?"

"Those prayers in your office? I sorted them. It took me years to isolate those level sevens, and you've probably never even looked at them."

God furrowed his brow, trying his best to conceal the fact that he didn't know what a level 7 was.

"Oh!" he said finally. "You're the one who sorted all the prayers."

Eliza nodded.

"In that case, I got a question. How come no one prays for field goals anymore? I used to love getting those. 'Please go in!' 'Please go wide!'" He chuckled.

Eliza took a deep breath and looked into her boss's eyes.

"Look," she said. "I know running Earth is hard. But if you're not going to try to fix things, if you're not going to really devote yourself to it, what's the point of being here? What's the point of even coming to work? Why not just quit?"

The room was so quiet, Eliza could hear herself breathing. Vince was glaring down at her, his nostrils flaring with contempt. Eliza wondered if she'd gone too far. She peered up at God, bracing herself for some kind of tirade. But the old man just smiled and nodded.

"You know what?" he said. "I've been thinking the same thing lately."

He turned to Vince. "If anyone calls, tell them I'm busy."

He put down his golf clubs. "I've got work to do."

Craig's eyes widened. "He canceled *golf?*"

He shook his head with a mixture of shock and admiration.

"I can't believe you just went up there and *talked* to him. I don't even like to make eye contact with the guy. One time we were about to pass each other in a hallway, and I got so nervous I hid inside the women's bathroom."

"It was a scary morning," Eliza acknowledged. "I mean, it's been five hours and my hands are still shaking! But sometimes, if you really want something, you've got to take risks. You know what I mean?"

Craig nodded unconvincingly. "Oh, I know!" he said. "Totally. *Risks.*"

He swiveled awkwardly toward his computer and checked his e-mail. There was a new message in his inbox—a company-wide memo from the CEO.

"Hey, Eliza!" he called out, through the wall of his cubicle. "Check your e-mail!"

He clicked on God's memo, leaning excitedly toward the screen.

Hey gang,

After much consideration I've decided to resign as CEO of Heaven Inc. It's been a fun ride, but part of being successful is knowing when to quit. I want to give a special thanks to Eliza Hunter from the Miracles Department, who really put things into perspective for me. Without her persuasive arguments, I might not have come to this decision.

The earth will be destroyed in a month. I haven't decided how to do it, but it will probably be by fire or by ice. (Demolition Dept.: I will make a decision soon, I promise!)

I realize that some of you might have questions about my decision. I've done my best to anticipate and answer them below:

You mentioned that the earth would be destroyed. Does that mean that you're also destroying heaven?

Of course not! We still have lots of xenon to collect. Even though I'm destroying the earth, its atmosphere will remain. I expect our collection numbers to stay as high as ever.

The humans, of course, will all be killed, so any jobs related to mankind will be eliminated.

My job was related to mankind. Where do I go now?

Usually, upon completing your term of service,

you would retire from heaven and rejoin Earth's population. Since there will no longer be an earth to return to, you will simply stay here from now on, in our beautiful corporate campus.

And don't worry. Even though your services are no longer needed, you will retain full access to our company's facilities. You don't have to turn in your bicycle. Your laundry will still be picked up on alternate Wednesdays. You'll still receive discounts at our gyms and snack bars—you'll just have more time to enjoy it all!

Do you really think it's necessary to destroy the earth and kill all of the humans?

Yes.

You've threatened to destroy the earth many times. In each instance, though, you've had a "last-second change of heart." Could something like that happen again?

I doubt it! It's not that I won't hear arguments—bring 'em on—but my mind is really made up about this thing. The planet's been on a downhill slide for centuries, and frankly I think it's time we cut our losses. Remember: in the grand scheme of our company, the earth and its creatures are not particularly significant.

What about our bonuses?

Everyone who was on track to receive a bonus for the third quarter of the fiscal year will receive the full amount, despite the shortened time frame. You're welcome!

Will any current humans come to heaven?

Possibly. But they won't be required to complete the usual term of service, since the Xenon Departments are full and the Earth-related jobs have been eliminated.

Isn't that a little unfair? We had to slave away in cubicles for years—why should these guys get a free ride?

I know it's a little unfair. But so is freezing or burning to death in the demolition of the earth! I think it balances out.

What are you going to do next?

I'm glad you asked! I'm pleased to announce that next month I will finally fulfill my lifelong dream of opening a restaurant. I'm calling it Sola, and we're going to specialize in Asian-American fusion.

I'm not super into Asian food. Is this restaurant for me?

While most of Sola's dishes have a Sichuan influence, our menu also includes some "comfort classics" that everyone can enjoy (steak frites, garlic roasted chicken, etc.).

How can I get a reservation at Sola?

Call the reservation desk any time from 9 a.m. to 5 p.m. Your party must be four or more.

"Holy shit!" Craig shouted, his eyes just inches from the screen. "Asian fusion? What the fuck is going on?"

He charged into Eliza's cubicle.

"Didn't I tell you not to go up there? Look what happened—look what you did!"

He kept on screaming until he realized she was crying.

"Eliza..."

He tried to pat her shoulder, but she shook him off.

"No," she murmured. "You're right. It's all my fault."

She covered her face with her hands. "I was just trying to help the humans. I ended up killing all of them."

She wiped her eyes with her sleeve. "What are we going to do now?"

"It's going to be okay," Craig said. "Everything's going to be okay."

A loud crash sounded from a nearby cubicle, followed by raucous laughter.

"Are people celebrating?" Eliza asked in disbelief.

Craig shook his head. "They probably just haven't heard the news yet."

Brian rode past them on an office chair, holding two beers. He was naked from the waist up.

"Have you heard the news? No more work!"

He offered Eliza one of the beers. She shook her head.

"Suit yourself." He took a sip from each beer and trundled down the hallway.

"I'm taking off my pants!" he announced. In the distance, people cheered.

"How can he be so drunk already?" Eliza wondered. "God only sent the memo fifteen minutes ago."

"It's amazing," Craig agreed.

"You need to talk to him."

"Oh, don't worry about Brian. He's got a crazy tolerance for alcohol."

"No. You need to talk to *God.*"

Craig laughed. "Me? I'm just some Angel. I can't walk into his office whenever I feel like it."

"I thought you said you had that kind of relationship."

Craig turned away.

"Come on," she pleaded. "We can't let him shut down our department!"

Craig thought about a miracle he was working on. A lost dog in Norway had wandered twenty miles from her owner. He had a plan to steer her back home, using a series of delicious airborne scents. He'd been so excited about the project—now he'd never get the chance to try it.

"Please," Eliza begged him. "The entire earth is counting on you."

"Why *me?*"

"Because you're the only Angel good enough to fix this. Nobody else on this floor could've rigged that piñata or cued that iPod..."

Craig squinted at her. "How'd you know about those?"

Eliza hesitated. "I snuck onto your computer," she admitted.

Craig's cheeks reddened slightly. "You liked those?"

She nodded firmly. "I loved them."

A surge of adrenaline coursed through Craig's bloodstream, as potent as a gallon of espresso.

"Okay," he heard himself say. "Okay. I'll go talk to him."

"You can't talk to him."

"Please, Vince. It's important."

"What department are you in again?"

"You know I'm in Miracles," Craig said. "In General Well-Being?"

Vince grinned. "Then how important could it possibly be?"

Craig winced. He didn't care if people insulted him personally; but when people insulted his *department,* it really stung. Sure, Miracles wasn't as important as, say, Gravity Enforcement or Ice Age Prevention. And, yeah, it wasn't as hip as Cloud Design or Peacock Production or the Department of Sunsets. And of course, technically, none of the human-related departments were as vital as Xenon Collection.

But Craig was proud of his little division. He would rather work in Miracles than anywhere else in heaven.

"What have you got against us?" he asked Vince. "You used to work on seventeen, remember?"

"Yeah," Vince said. "Before my promotion."

"Is it okay if I sit in the waiting area?" Craig begged. "Until God's free?"

Vince shrugged.

"Knock yourself out."

Vince Blake squinted at the chunky, unkempt Angel in his waiting area. He'd hated Craig for as long as he could remember. They'd started out in Miracles at the same time; they'd even taken their introductory tour together. But it was clear from the start that they were very different people.

Vince, for instance, hated being an Angel. The endless research, the tedious coding, the maddening anonymity. He could still remember Craig's first miracle: he'd spent forty-eight hours weakening a plank of wood with termites so that a scrawny girl would be able to chop through it at her karate exhibition. When the kid smacked the board and it crumbled apart, the entire floor burst into applause. Some of the senior Angels started chanting Craig's name, like he'd cured cancer or something.

"That was beautiful, Craig—just beautiful!"

It was ridiculous—who cared about some random girl's karate class? How could they devote so much time to something so trivial?

Most Angels viewed themselves as artists, delicate craftsmen striving for elegance. Their goal was to remain as invisible as possible, to change the world with subtlety and grace. Vince thought they were a bunch of pussies. On his very first day on seventeen, he made a private vow: he would only design miracles that were bold, loud, and guaranteed to get press coverage.

In his first month on the job, he gave an infertile woman in Boise sextuplets. His colleagues warned him about the health risks and tried to convince him to lower the number of babies. He responded by adding two more babies to the mix, making it the first octuplet birth in medical history. The other Angels called the stunt "sloppy" and "reckless." But Vince didn't care. The *New York Post* had called it a miracle.

One week later he made a Brazilian statue of the Virgin Mary weep tears of blood. He was suspended for three days, but he returned more brazen than ever. On a sunny afternoon in May, he guided a flock of geese into the path of a 747 jet. As the plane plummeted from the sky, he weaved it between two skyscrapers and directed it into the Hudson River. There were dozens of injuries but no fatalities—making it the most "miraculous" crash landing in memory. The event was so spectacular, even the media had to acknowledge heaven's hand.

"Miracle on the Hudson!" raved the tabloids.

It was God's best press in years. As soon as he saw the headlines, he gave Vince a promotion to the executive wing, where he'd been ever since.

Vince squinted across the room at Craig. He was disgusted by the Angel's physical appearance. His coffee-stained khakis clung unflatteringly to his hips and his wrinkled blue Oxford was missing at least one button. His filthy brown hair was speckled with visible dandruff flakes. He wore socks with his sandals and the socks didn't even match.

The men accidentally made eye contact, and Craig ventured a smile. But the Archangel just glared at him. Craig was one of the pretentious snobs who had criticized his octuplet miracle. Vince had overheard him talking about it in the break room—he'd called it a piece of "hackwork." Craig probably didn't remember saying it, but Vince would never forget it.

The Archangel was so lost in his thoughts, he failed to notice his boss's arrival. "If it's about the bonuses," God was saying to Craig, "I already explained it in the memo."

"It's not about the bonuses!" Craig promised.

Vince quickly stepped between them.

"Can't you see he's busy?" he snarled at Craig. "If you have any questions about the earth—"

"This isn't about the earth," Craig lied. "It's about...uh...it's about the restaurant."

Vince stared at him incredulously.

"I think Asian fusion is the future," Craig said. "I want to get in on the ground floor."

God raised his eyebrows. "Are you telling me you'd like to *invest?*"

Craig sighed. "Yes," he said. "I would like to invest."

God threw a meaty arm over Craig's shoulder and walked him down the hall, past an astonished Vince.

"You won't regret this!" God said. "You and me are going straight to the top!"

"Some places *say* they're Asian fusion," God said. "But really they're just watered-down Chinese. I'm talking about taking the pan-Asian experience and enhancing it with classic Western ingredients. Lemongrass French fries! Fish sauce spaghetti! Nobody's doing this but me."

"It sounds really great," Craig said.

"You're damn right it sounds great! I just came up with it yesterday, and I already think it's my best project ever."

"Better than mankind?"

God rolled his eyes. "Much better."

Craig looked at the clock. They'd been talking about Sola for nearly two hours. It was time to make his move.

"You know, God, I didn't come up here just to talk about Sola."

God raised his eyebrows. "You didn't?"

"I mean—that was a big part of it. But also, I was thinking...maybe you shouldn't give up on the earth just yet."

God flicked his wrist dismissively.

"That project's a bust. I'm not throwing more good time after bad."

"I know things are rough down there. But don't you think you could make it better?"

"Look," God said. "Since we're going into business together, I'm gonna level with you. With that whole mankind thing? I bit off *way more* than I could chew."

He gestured at his overflowing inbox.

"You know, I've never answered a single human prayer? It's not that I haven't tried—I used to spend ten minutes a day on those suckers. I just could never get them to work."

Craig stared at his boss with astonishment. "Not even little prayers?"

God shook his head.

"Last year this guy prayed for me to fix his stereo antenna. I tried to help him out—ended up striking him in the face with lightning. Two times—*bap bap!* He exploded."

"Why didn't you just modulate the radio waves? You know, with an electrical code?"

"I've never been big on computers," God admitted. "I tried to get Vince to teach me the YouTube, but after a minute or two I thought, 'Who needs it?'"

"You know," Craig said, "I'm pretty good with computers. I bet I could answer some of those prayers for you, if you gave me a chance."

God smirked. "I doubt it."

"I'm serious. In the Miracles Department, we deal with these types of things all the time."

"Remind me which one Miracles is?"

"We're on the seventeenth floor?"

God stared at him blankly.

"We reunited Lynyrd Skynyrd?"

"Oh, yeah!" God said. "That was great. But they were probably going to get back together anyway."

Craig was trying to be polite, but he could feel his voice rising with frustration.

"Things aren't as hopeless as you're making them out to be. Come down to seventeen—I'll show you some of my miracles. I've done hundreds of them. I did two this morning! I helped a guy in Alaska strike oil, I won a girl a stuffed bear at Coney Island..."

"How do I know those weren't just coincidences?"

Craig clenched his fists in his lap. "What do I have to do to convince you?"

God folded his arms. "You've gotta call your shot."

He pushed his giant inbox across the desk.

"This thing's full of prayers. Pick one—any one. It can be the easiest prayer in the whole box. If you tell me you can solve it—and you do it by next month—I'll keep the earth open."

Craig's eyes widened. "Seriously?"

"Sure, kid. Show me how it's done!"

God reached across the table, grabbed Craig's hand, and shook it.

"Now," he said. "How much were you thinking of investing?"

"All you have to do is answer one prayer? And he'll save the earth?"

Craig nodded spastically.

"We *shook* on it!"

He stared at God's inbox, a heavy brass tray overflowing with prayers. It was so gigantic it barely fit on his desk. Craig riffled through the stack and Eliza started coughing from the dust.

"There are so many," he said. "How am I going to pick one?"

"What about this one?" Eliza suggested. "It's only a two."

"What's a two?"

Eliza explained the Urgency Scale to Craig.

"That's a smart system," he said. "Who came up with it?"

Eliza blushed. "I did."

She self-consciously adjusted her bangs, running her fingers through her soft brown hair.

Craig hesitated. There was something he wanted to ask her, but he wasn't sure how to do it.

"Hey," he said, "I was thinking...since you know

so much about prayers—and I know about miracles—maybe it would be a good idea if..."

Eliza nodded. "I'd love to help."

"Really?"

"Sure! It'd be fun to collaborate on something for a change. And also, you know, it would be nice to save the world."

He beamed at her. "We should start right now—there isn't a lot of time."

"Fine by me."

"Hey...do you like pizza?"

"Of course. Why?"

Craig smiled proudly. "I've got a coupon."

"I think these are your best bet," Eliza told Craig, handing him a short stack.

Craig put down his slice and flipped through them. "You didn't give me much to choose from."

Eliza shrugged. "Almost everything in this inbox is expired. Look."

She handed him a yellowed scrap of paper from the bottom of the pile.

Dear God: Please get me tickets to C+C Music Factory.
Tania Banks, March 3, 1991

"Are they all like that?" Craig asked.

Eliza nodded. "These are the only recent ones."

She handed him the prayers, and he carefully laid them out across his desk.

"Okay," he said. "Let's look at our options."

Dear God: please give my fat boss a heart attack.
Joseph Hickey, 38, Northern Ireland

"Could be tricky," Craig said. "I could build up plaque in the guy's arteries, but I doubt that would kill him by next month."

"He's already fat—that might make it easier."

Craig nodded. "Good point."

He went to his computer and located the boss in question. He was pacing down the hallway of his Belfast office, screaming at all the underlings in his path.

Craig shook his head with disappointment. "He's not that fat."

Eliza pointed to the next prayer. "What about this one?"

Please let the Mariners win the pennant for once in my fucking life.
Mike Bear, 42, Seattle

"I don't know," Craig said. "Sports are tough."

"How tough can they be?"

"God's a die-hard Yankees fan. He's got six Archangels working on them every day—driving their fly balls fair, injuring their opponents. And they *still* win only about sixty percent of their games. It's not worth the risk."

He picked up the next prayer:

Dear God: Please don't let my hamster die.
Andrea Oran, 7, St. Louis

Craig zoomed in on the little girl's bedroom. Her hamster lay in the corner of a fetid cage, taking rapid, shallow breaths. Craig shook his head.

"That hamster's a goner."

They shuffled through the remaining prayers, their anxiety rapidly mounting. Everyone wanted the impossible: a Mega Millions jackpot, a perfect SAT score, a pony. Eventually, they were down to their last prayer. Craig took a deep breath and unfolded it.

It was a recent plea from a twenty-two-year-old New Yorker.

Please let me and Laura be together.
Sam Katz, March 23, 2011

Craig banged his desk with frustration.

"What's wrong with that one?" Eliza asked.

"Love miracles are impossible," he said. "I've tried them—they never work."

"Why not?"

"You can't make two humans fall in love with each other. Too many variables."

"Like what?"

"This Laura girl could be married, for all we know. Just because you love someone doesn't mean they'll ever love you back."

He picked up the prayer from Seattle. "How many games back are the Mariners?"

Eliza shrugged. "I have no idea."

They sat for a minute in silence.

"Hey—why is this one two pages?"

He handed Eliza the love prayer, and she realized there was a second sheet stapled to it. She hadn't noticed it at first; the pages had languished in God's inbox for so long, they'd gotten stuck together.

"That just means there's a duplicate," she explained. "Identical prayers are stapled together to save God time."

"So someone else wants Sam to get this Laura girl."

Eliza nodded.

"Probably one of his buddies."

She unstapled the pages with a paper clip and read the first one out loud. " 'Please let me and Laura be together. Sam.' "

"What's the second page say?"

Eliza's eyes widened with excitement.

"What?" Craig said. "Come on, read it."

"'Please let me and *Sam* be together. Laura.'"

The Angels made eye contact and grinned.

"You want to know something?" Craig said. "That could work."

God passed Craig a book of carpet samples. "I can't decide between the turquoise and the teal."

Craig nodded, his eyebrows furrowed to feign interest. "Is this for the main dining area?"

"No," God said. "The vestibule. When you first walk into the restaurant."

Craig flipped through the color options. "I think the teal," he said.

"Really?"

"Call me crazy, but I think it fits the mood. Especially if you're going with beige for the tablecloths. You know—they're both nice, muted colors."

God nodded. "That's a good point."

He picked up his phone and dialed an extension.

"Vince? I'm pulling the trigger on the vestibule carpet. That's right. We're going teal!"

He stood up.

"Well, I guess that's everything," he said proudly.

Craig hesitated. "Actually, I was wondering—is it cool if we maybe talk for a second about that Earth thing?"

God sat back down.

"I forgot about that. What's up?"

Craig slid the pair of prayers across the desk.

"I'm calling my shot," he said.

God squinted at the two slips of paper. "The wording's a little vague. I mean, 'be together'? That could mean anything."

"I don't think it's vague. It just means these two humans want to become a couple."

"Well, yeah, but at what moment do two people 'become a couple'?"

"I guess I don't know," Craig conceded. "What do you think?"

God shrugged. "Intercourse?"

Craig coughed. "I don't think that's fair," he said. "I mean, that's a lot to arrange in a month. How about this: we'll say the prayer's been answered if they go out on a date?"

God considered his proposal.

"I think it's gotta be intercourse," he said.

Craig sighed.

"How about a kiss," he suggested.

God stroked his chin. "What kind of kiss? We talking tongue?"

Craig shook his head. "Let's just say, on the lips. The prayer's been answered if they kiss on the lips sometime in the next thirty days."

God thought about it.

"Okay," he said, thrusting out his hand. "Deal."

Craig shook God's hand—and saw that his boss was laughing.

"What's so funny?"

"It's never going to work."

Craig shifted uncomfortably in his seat.

"How hard could it be?" he said. "They already want to be together. All I have to do is give them an opportunity."

"Just because you give the humans something doesn't mean they'll take advantage of it. They're like goldfish. You can drop something right in front of their faces and they'll just ignore it. Do you know how long it was before the humans tried fruit? Like, a thousand years. For a while they just walked up to the trees, poked at them with sticks, and ran away."

"Why?"

"Because they're afraid of *everything*. It's their biggest defect. Other than the dying thing."

"Maybe those two are related?"

"Oooh, Mr. Philosophy!"

Craig looked down at his lap, embarrassed.

"Well," he mumbled. "I'll keep you posted."

"No need," God told him. "I'll be watching."

Eliza was sitting at her desk, waiting for Craig to return, when she heard screaming. It was coming from a cubicle down the hall. She ran toward the sound, assuming a colleague was hurt. But she quickly realized the noise was coming from a computer. Brian had left his desk in Physical Safety unattended.

She stepped into Brian's empty cubicle and peered at

his screen. A suburban teenager was writhing next to a trampoline, clutching his ankle in agony.

"Whoops," Brian said, as he walked back from the bathroom. "Probably shouldn't have left."

"Is he badly hurt?" Eliza asked.

Brian glanced at the screen and laughed.

"Oh, yeah," he said. He closed the window.

"Man," he said. "I am *hung* over."

He took a family-size tub of Alka-Seltzer out of his filing cabinet and shook some tablets onto his desk. The bottle, Eliza noticed, was almost empty.

"You want to know something?" Brian said. "I'm a bad Angel."

"I'm sure that's not true."

"No, it's true," Brian said. "I am really bad at my job. You know how many injuries I've prevented this quarter? Two. And they were both paper cuts. Can you believe that? Two miracles in three months!"

He squinted at Eliza, seeming to register her presence for the first time since she'd arrived in the department.

"Has anyone given you a tour yet?" he asked.

"Craig showed me the whole floor, General Well-Being, Physical Safety—"

"That's not a tour," Brian interrupted. "The company's more than just offices. We've got a whole badass *campus* at our disposal. The only company on Earth that comes close to this place is Google. And in my opinion, we've got them beat."

He tossed two Alka-Seltzer tablets into a bottle of water and waited for the liquid to fizz.

"This heaven place has everything. Did you know there's a sushi counter next to the beach volleyball court? It's open twenty-four hours a day. If you show your wings, it's free."

He pointed at her sternly. "Ask for the double dragon roll. If you order anything else, you're a moron."

Eliza nodded.

"That's just the tip of the iceberg," Brian said. "Every Tuesday there's massages in the pavilion. Find Lucy—she knows what she's doing. She's usually there from two till four."

"Aren't those business hours?"

Brian laughed. "Nobody cares if you skip work. Last month I took eleven personal days. Nobody said a word."

He smirked. "Craig probably didn't even tell you we *got* personal days."

"He didn't," she admitted.

"He never takes advantage of this place."

"Maybe that's because he's too busy doing important work."

"Come on," Brian said. "We're not important. No matter how many miracles we pull off, it's barely a drop in the ocean. This whole office is ridiculous. Honestly, I can't wait for it to shut down."

"Maybe you're just in the wrong department."

Brian shook his head. "They're all bummers. Trust me—I've been everywhere."

"Where else have you worked?"

Brian whistled. "Where do I start? I used to be in Geyser Regulation. That was a real nightmare. You literally do the same thing every day. And if you're off by even five minutes, everyone *freaks out.*"

"That does sound kind of rough."

"Not as rough as Volcano Suppression. Talk about a thankless job. You work a twenty-hour shift, stop a thousand volcanoes from erupting. And the next day, the only thing people want to talk about is the one you missed. Also, that was back before we got computers—so I had to map out everything by *hand.* With slide rules and protractors and these flimsy charcoal pencils. I was able to get a transfer, but then they stuck me in Beaches. And that's when things *really* got bad."

He shuddered slightly at the memory.

"I spent *five years* turning sand into glass," he said. "Can you imagine? Sand into glass, sand into glass, sand into glass."

He gulped down his Alka-Seltzer.

"Are there any departments that deal with important stuff?" Eliza asked.

"Like what?"

"I don't know. Like, sickness and famine and death?"

"Oh. There's the Department of Dire Situations—but it's still in the experimental phase. The office is right next to the steam baths, and whenever I walk by, I hear people running around and yelling at each other. I don't think anyone likes it there."

Eliza nodded, slightly dazed. The company was so vast it was impossible to visualize it all.

"I gotta tell you," Brian said. "If it wasn't for the Server, I'd probably have gone insane by now."

"What Server?"

Brian gaped at her. "Are you serious? Craig didn't even show you how to work the Server?"

Eliza shook her head. "He didn't even mention it."

Brian rolled his eyes. "Of course he didn't."

He dragged a second chair into the cubicle.

"Sit down," he commanded. "We're going to have some fun."

The Server was a complicated piece of software, but its function was simple: to record everything that ever happened on Earth. By throwing a few keywords into the mainframe, you could watch any event in human history, from any angle, in fast-forward, rewind, or freeze-frame. The program was invented for research purposes, but the Angels used it for one thing and one thing only: procrastination.

"Come on," Brian said. "I'll show you how Lincoln gets shot."

"That's so *morbid,*" Eliza said, but she could feel herself inching closer to the screen.

Brian typed "Ford's Theater Washington DC," "Abraham Lincoln," and "1865" into a search box. A few different windows popped up; apparently, Lincoln had attended several shows that year.

"We want this one," Brian said, clicking on the box with the latest date.

Eliza watched in rapt silence as Brian zoomed in on the theater's red-brick roof. The roof grew in size on the screen, then suddenly disappeared, replaced by a grid of balding scalps and floral bonnets. They were inside the theater, looking down on the audience.

Brian tilted the view slightly so they could see the stage.

"Let's skip ahead," he said, clicking on the fast-forward icon.

The actors buzzed back and forth across the clapboard stage, gesturing rapidly. The audience clapped and laughed in unison.

"Here it comes," Brian said.

He zoomed in on a roped-off area in the upper balcony. At first Eliza thought Brian had selected the wrong box; it was empty except for an unattractive elderly couple. But as he zoomed in closer she realized that they were the Lincolns. She hadn't recognized them. She'd seen paintings of them before, but they looked so different in real life.

Brian unclicked fast-forward, and they watched the Lincolns watch the play in real time. Mary Todd was a lot heavier than Eliza had expected (the portrait artists had obviously been kind). Her flabby neck glistened with sweat, and she kept dabbing at it with a coarse beige handkerchief. There was a small black hair growing out of a mole on her cheek, and she picked at it from time to time, never quite extracting it. The president never laughed at the play, but he smiled genially throughout the second act. His eyes were damp and deeply sunken in his pale, crinkled face.

Suddenly a sweaty man appeared behind the couple, holding a small black derringer. He was surprisingly handsome. He paused for a moment, then slowly raised the gun to Lincoln's head.

"I can't watch!" Eliza shouted, covering her eyes. When she next looked at the screen, the president was lying on the rug, a murky red puddle pooling horribly by his skull.

"Want to watch it in slo-mo?" Brian asked, shaking some more Alka-Seltzer onto his desk.

Eliza shook her head. "Could we maybe switch it to something... less horrible?"

"Sure," Brian said. "We can watch whatever we want."

Before Eliza knew it, they had spent three hours surfing the Server. They watched the first Beatles rehearsal (surprisingly boring) and Mozart's first recital at Versailles (disappointingly brief). They watched Joan of Arc give a rambling speech to a pack of worried soldiers. They watched Nefertiti take a bath—an outrageously complicated process, which took them twenty minutes to get through, even in fast-forward. Eliza grimaced as the English let loose on the Spanish Armada, torching their ships and scorching their sailors. She laughed at an Athenian dwarf as he tumbled crazily across a sunlit marble stage.

But the most absorbing discovery was something she found by accident. She was watching some seventeenth-century Indians trap beavers when she clicked the zoom out icon. The Indians shrank down to specks, and jagged coastlines appeared on all sides.

"What's that little island?" she asked, pointing at the rectangular strip of land.

"That's Manhattan," he said. "See?"

He clicked fast-forward, and the city began to take shape. First a cluster of houses spread messily across the island's southern tip. Then came cobblestone streets, cutting through the forest like a pack of silver snakes, eating all the trees in their path.

"Can we go faster?"

Brian clicked the ×500 icon, and a grid of roads cut brutally through the forest, followed by a smattering of farmhouses. The blur of horses swelled—then vanished—replaced by a smudge of cars. Downtown the city rose, then burned, then rose again—this time in steel and glass. Planes popped suddenly into the frame, clogging the sky, obscuring the view. And then the action suddenly came to a stop. They'd reached the present moment.

"Look at all the people," Eliza whispered, zooming in on Times Square. "I mean, honestly...there's no way to help them all."

Brian laughed. "Don't worry," he said. "They never know the difference."

"And then we watched the *Titanic* go down!" Eliza told Craig breathlessly. "There was this Irish guy—he was dressed up as a woman. And when they confronted him on the lifeboat, he spoke in this crazy high-pitched voice, like, 'Oh, heavens! I'm just a wee lady!' "

Craig nodded. "I've seen that."

"You know the band didn't actually 'play on,' like people say. They pretty much just screamed and panicked like everyone else. Two of them *tried* to dress up as women, but they couldn't find bonnets. Then we watched Oscar Wilde die! Get this: they say his last words were 'Either this wallpaper goes or I do'—but actually he said, 'I need more morphine and someone needs to wash my ass.' Not so witty, huh? What else...oh! Helen of Troy wasn't really that pretty. And Paul Revere never warned anyone about the British! He just told people that's where he was going, because he was too afraid to stick around and fight!"

She noticed that Craig was ignoring her.

"Craig? What's wrong?"

He shrugged. "Nothing."

"You sure?"

"I'm fine."

He turned on his computer and stared in silence at the load screen.

"You know...it's not always a great idea to watch stuff like that on the Server."

She saluted sarcastically. "I know, I know. 'Research only.'"

"It's not that," he said, his eyes still on the screen. "It's just..."

He faced her. "It'll make you feel bad, you know? It'll make you cynical."

Eliza noticed with shock that Craig's eyes were a bit shiny, almost like he was trying to hold back tears.

"I'm sorry," she whispered. "I shouldn't have talked about it so much."

Craig forced a laugh, embarrassed. "It's fine!" he said. "No big deal! I'm just *exhausted*, you know...I'm just tired."

He dragged a sleeve roughly across his face. "What do you say we get to work?"

Eliza smiled softly at him. "That sounds great, Craig."

Computers in the Miracles Department came equipped with several powerful search engines. There was Omnex, which allowed Angels to locate specific humans.

There was RoomScanner, which allowed them to find missing objects. There was Hydrosearch for drinking wells and Gushspot for oil and Google for news. But Craig's favorite tool by far was ComCheck.

ComCheck—short for "compatibility check"—was an impressive piece of computer engineering. By measuring thousands of key variables, it calculated with perfect certainty how happy two people would make each other over the course of their lifetimes. "Never try to link two humans," the manual warned, "unless you've run ComCheck first."

"It's no wonder they're in love," Craig said. "Look."

He typed Sam's and Laura's names into the computer, pressed F4, and waited for the results to tabulate. When the numbers came in, Eliza whistled with excitement. Compatibility scores ranged from 0 ("inevitable murder-suicide") to 100 ("guaranteed bliss"). Sam and Laura scored 96. They had identical senses of humor and the same taste in furniture. They shared a fondness for garlic and a hatred of mushrooms. They were physically attracted to each other, and even though Sam was predisposed to baldness, Laura found that trait endearing. They even liked different flavors of Life Savers, so if they ever bought a pack at a movie theater, there would be no quarreling or resentment. The only thing keeping them from a perfect score was Sam's deviated septum: Laura was a light sleeper, and his snoring was sure to wake her up occasionally. But that could be corrected someday, with minor surgery.

"How did they meet?" Eliza asked.

"I'll show you," Craig said.

He typed "Sam Katz AND Laura Potts" into the Server and clicked on the earliest link.

EARTH—SEPTEMBER 4, 2007

Laura Potts read about the protest on the activities board. The flyer was red and enormous.

> Every two hours, a Bangladeshi child is murdered in a factory for no reason.
>
> Do something about it.
>
> Saturday at noon.
>
> 14th Street and Broadway.

She questioned the flyer's accuracy (that statistic added up to twelve murdered children each day). But she couldn't stomach another day of solitude, another day of eating granola bars from the vending machine and debating whether to call her mother. She had skipped the Sigma Nu party and slept through the

Statue of Liberty trip. It was the last day of freshman orientation, and this protest was her last chance to make friends, possibly ever.

So far college had been a disaster. She shared a six-person suite with five recruited field hockey players, monstrous, horselike women who hogged the shower and wielded sticks wherever they went. She'd tried to talk to them, but they were always rushing off to the gym or the dining hall, and they never seemed to hear her. She was constantly repeating herself, over and over again, in every conversation.

"Hey, I'm Laura from Athens, Georgia."

"What?"

"Athens!"

"What?"

"The South!"

"Oh."

These exchanges worried her. Was her accent so unusual? Was her voice so faint?

Her two closest friends had gone to the University of Georgia. She wanted to call them but was afraid she would start to cry over the phone. Instead, she sent them short, controlled e-mails that she wrote in the style of a New York City guidebook. "There are so many amazing restaurants," her last one raved. "You could eat at a different one each night for your entire life and still not try them all!" In truth, she had been to only one restaurant, a shockingly expensive Japanese place with ridiculous tin menus. She went on her second night at school with a large group of freshmen. The waiter made her repeat her order six times and eventually asked her to write it down on a piece of paper. She sat across from a boy from Los Angeles and a girl from Connecticut who talked about books she hadn't heard of. During the first minute of the conversation, Laura lied about having read *Siddhartha* and spent the rest of the meal visualizing what would happen if she got caught. By the time dessert came, the boy and girl were talking about politics and their ankles were entwined beneath the table. Laura sat in silence, praying someone would speak to her. After ten mute minutes, a nervous boy tapped her on the shoulder. She swiveled toward him, smiling brightly.

"Hey!" she said. "What's up?"

"If you had sake," he mumbled, "then it's seventy-eight dollars."

On the morning of the protest, Laura got up early and put in her contact lenses. She was determined to socialize, even if it meant joining the Bangladeshi cause. She put on her most "alternative" sweatshirt, a brown hemp hoodie, and on the short walk to Fourteenth Street, she resolved to make at least one friend.

Laura knew she'd made a mistake when she saw the protest leader. She was standing on an upturned bucket, beating a large, misshapen drum. Her dress was black and sack-shaped, and she was screaming.

"There are four thousand child slaves toiling in Bangladeshi factories! They toil at their looms for eighteen hours a day in sweltering, windowless bunkers. If a child leaves his workstation he is *shot in the face* by a member of the Chittagong Army! Is that justice?"

The crowd yelled "No!" in unison.

"He is *shot* in the *face!*" the woman emphasized.

Laura realized with panic that everyone but her was wearing black. Her armpits prickled with perspiration. The flyer hadn't said anything about a dress code.

She took a deep breath and marched intrepidly into the fray. A glowering girl made eye contact with her, and Laura seized the opportunity, blurting out her standard introduction.

"Hi, I'm Laura!"

The girl handed her a flyer and kept on walking, shuffling her way through the crowd. Laura noticed that the back of the girl's shirt pictured the face of a screaming Bangladeshi child. Beneath the child, in red block letters, a caption read simply: "Justice?" She wondered how quickly she could leave without appearing to be insensitive.

A bony palm gripped her shoulder. When she turned around, an emaciated girl was addressing her in a squeaky falsetto. "Is this your first die-in?"

Laura swallowed. Had she inadvertently joined some kind of suicide pact?

"What's a die-in?"

"It's when you simulate death," the girl explained. "To protest the unjust deaths of others."

A large gong sounded, and the skinny girl's eyes suddenly widened.

"It's starting!"

Laura watched in horror as the screaming protest leader unfurled a banner ("This many Bangladeshi children are murdered each week"). And before she had time to think, she was lying on the filthy sidewalk, her right check pressed into the pavement.

Several feet away, Sam Katz shifted uncomfortably and tried to make sense of his situation. He didn't even know what this particular protest was about. He had been on his way to the library when an enraged girl thrust a flyer in his face.

"Do you care whether children live or die?"

Sam flinched. "I guess I'd rather they live?"

"Then do something!"

She muscled him into the center of the crowd, and the next thing he knew he was lying on the ground, surrounded by strangers and lonelier than ever. He'd been at NYU for a whole week, and this five-second exchange with the protester was the longest conversation he'd had yet.

Near his face a loudspeaker blasted a Bangladeshi song. It was loud, atonal, and full of screaming.

"Takana! Murti! Takana!"

It was crazy music and Sam realized, with panic, that

it was going to make him laugh. He bit his lip. He'd been working so hard to pass himself off as a real New Yorker; yawning at the sight of tall buildings, ignoring celebrities on the street, writing in his Moleskine notebook, and sneering whenever anyone smiled at him. It seemed to be working. But if he laughed right now, in front of all of these smart political types, his Oklahoma origins would be plain for all to see.

"Takana! Takana! Takana!"

Sam clenched his jaw. The instruments had cut out—and now the song was just pure a cappella screaming. He could feel the laughter rising uncontrollably in his throat, as unstoppable as a pepper sneeze. He was about to give up the fight when he heard a high-pitched giggle coming from about six feet away. He craned his neck and spotted a girl wearing an odd brown sweatshirt, with her hands clamped tightly over her mouth. She flashed him an embarrassed smile, and he smiled right back, forgetting that he was supposed to sneer, forgetting he was in New York, forgetting practically everything.

"That's it?" Eliza asked. "That's the whole clip?"

Craig nodded. "That's it."

"What ended up happening? You know, after the protest?"

"The Chittagong Army continued to gain strength," Craig told her. "Their atrocities continue to this day."

"No," Eliza said. "I mean, what happened with Sam and Laura?"

"Oh. Nothing."

"They didn't talk after the protest?"

Craig shook his head. "Their next meeting isn't for another eight months. Here it is—Fifteenth Street and Irving."

He clicked on the link, and Eliza shifted impatiently in her seat, waiting for the clip to start.

EARTH—MAY 12, 2008

Sam stood across the street from Irving Plaza, trying to breathe like a normal person. He'd spotted Laura twenty minutes ago, through the plate-glass window of a gyro shop, and he was determined to finally speak to her. It wasn't his first opportunity—they'd shared a dining hall for months. But the odds were it was his last chance of the year. Classes had ended on Friday, and he was flying home to Tulsa at six the next morning. If he didn't make his move right now, who knew when he'd get another shot?

He rehearsed his opening line under his breath a few times, debating various deliveries. Finally, he walked across the street and tapped her on the shoulder.

"Hey," he said. "You in line for the show?"

Laura nodded. She'd been watching Sam for about ten

minutes, trying to figure out why he kept mumbling under his breath. She'd wanted to meet him ever since the protest but hadn't had the guts to approach him.

"I love the Fuzz," Sam said. "They're kind of reminiscent of early Brian Eno."

Laura smiled confusedly. She'd never heard of Brian Eno. She was debating whether to feign agreement with him when the line started moving.

"Guess it's starting," she said, shuffling along with the crowd.

"Oh!" Sam said. "Okay. Well... sayonara!"

She waved awkwardly. "Bye!"

Sam shook his head wearily. He'd finally worked up the courage to talk to her, after months of campus stalking, and it had gone all wrong. Why had he said that thing about Brian Eno? And "sayonara"? What the hell was that? The conversation had been such an unmitigated disaster he almost felt like laughing. His only solace was that nobody had been around to see it.

"Man," Eliza said. "That was hard to watch."

Craig nodded. "Did you see how much he was sweating?"

"I didn't notice."

Craig hit the pause button and zoomed in on Sam's oil-drenched forehead.

"And this is at night," Craig marveled. "He's sweating like this at *night*."

"What the hell was that Brian Eno thing about?"

"I'll show you."

Craig closed the clip and opened one from twenty minutes earlier. Sam was sitting in the gyro stand across the street from Irving Plaza, scrutinizing a listing in the *Village Voice.*

"It looks like he's reading the same article over and over again," Eliza said.

"He is."

Craig paused the clip, adjusted the angle, and zoomed in on the newspaper.

> The Fuzz rocks Irving Plaza Sunday with a sound reminiscent of early Brian Eno.

Eliza cringed. "So he was just repeating what the *paper* said?"

Craig nodded. "He's never heard a single Brian Eno song. I checked his entire Life History."

"Wow." She closed her eyes. "Remember when he said 'sayonara'?"

Craig shuddered. "I don't want to talk about that."

He scrolled down to the humans' next meeting.

"I haven't watched the third one yet. Maybe it goes better?"

"When's it from?"

"Two years later—spring of 2010."

She covered her eyes. "I'm afraid to watch."

"We've got to."

He clicked on the link, and the clip began to roll.

EARTH—APRIL 3, 2010

"Hey," Laura said. "You're in Linguistics Twelve, right?"

Sam nodded.

"Are those responses due today?"

Sam nodded.

"Okay," she said. "Um... thanks!"

Eliza threw her hands up in frustration.

"What the fuck was that?"

Craig shrugged. "I guess they're both shy."

She shook her head in disgust. "She came right up to him, initiated a conversation, and he didn't even say a word."

"He was panicking. See? Look at all that sweat."

He paused the clip and zoomed in tight on Sam's glistening neck.

"I wonder if he has a medical condition," Craig mused. "Like a gland thing."

"Does she even know his name at this point?" Eliza wondered.

"Probably not."

"So how do they fall in love? When does it happen?"

"Not in 2010. That's their last meeting for the entire year."

He scrolled down to the next link.

"Hey, this is interesting," she said. "This next clip's four hours long."

She clicked on the link, and the Bobst Library appeared on the screen. Someone had called in a bomb threat, and students were idling outside, talking, laughing, thankful for the break.

From a bird's-eye angle you could see that Sam's hair had started thinning. Laura's posture, always bad, had stooped markedly since the year before. They were getting older.

Even though they were standing right next to each other, it took them three whole minutes to achieve eye contact and another four to speak to each other.

The Angels watched patiently as the humans began to make small talk.

"Do you know Max?" Laura tried. *"I think he was in your dorm."*

Sam squinted. *"Max Feldman?"*

Laura shook her head. *"Max Padrick."*

"Oh. No, I don't think I know him."

Eliza groaned.

"This conversation is so *boring.*"

"We could watch it in fast-forward?" Craig suggested.

Eliza nodded, and he clicked the ×50 icon.

The humans chattered rapidly while the crowd thinned around them. Eventually, Sam and Laura were the only ones left on the steps. Their eye contact remained glancing, but their expressions grew brighter, their hand gestures more animated.

Craig hit play at the twenty-minute mark and found that their conversation had shifted from mutual acquaintances to reality television.

"They're making progress."

Eliza shrugged. "Barely."

Craig hit ×1,000, and the humans scurried up Broadway, darting into a nearby diner. The first laugh occurred just after the one-hour mark, followed by two more in quick succession. Sam and Laura stayed in their booth for hours, drinking iced coffee, the only stationary figures in a blur of whirling activity.

Eventually the humans darted outside, zigzagging aimlessly until they reached a bench by the Hudson River. A hundred cars a minute whizzed by them on the West Side Highway, an electric blur of red and yellow streaks. Gradually, the humans started to inch toward each other on the bench. In real time, the shift was imperceptible—too gradual for Sam and Laura to be aware of it. But watching in fast-forward, the Angels could make out their progress. By the three-hour-and-forty-one-minute mark, their knees were practically touching.

Suddenly, though, there was a dramatic shift in body language. Sam retreated to the far end of the bench, like a losing prizefighter at the bell—his eyes downcast, his shoulders drooping.

"What was that?" Eliza asked.

"Not sure."

Craig rewound the clip a bit and then hit play so they could figure out what happened.

EARTH—MARCH 23, 2011

Sam and Laura sat on the bench, their eyes locked.

"I don't get Kerouac either," Laura said. "I mean, I know he's supposed to be smart and everything, but I just get bored reading it."

"I feel the same way!" Sam said. "You know, I've never told that to anyone."

"Me neither! I've always just pretended to like him because—"

"You were afraid of what they'd say."

"Exactly! Oh my God, if Cliff ever heard me badmouthing Kerouac..."

"Who's Cliff?"

"Um...he's...my...boyfriend."

"Whoa."

"That *sucks.*"

Craig paced around the cubicle, clenching his fists in outrage.

"She waited *four hours* to tell him she had a boyfriend? That's *inexcusable.*"

"What about *him?* He waited four hours to *ask.*"

Craig shook his head. "The blame's on her. No question. Because *that—*" He pointed at the screen. "*That* was *bullshit.*"

He sat back down and rewound the clip. "Let's watch it in slow motion."

Eliza covered her eyes. "I can't—it's worse than when Lincoln gets shot."

Craig ignored her and played Laura's confession at one-tenth speed. Her voice rumbled out of the computer speaker, slow and deep.

"Um..."

Her pupils shifted back and forth.

"He's..."

She tilted her head downward.

"My..."

Craig shifted the angle on the clip so they could watch Sam's reaction.

"Boy...friend."

Craig hit freeze-frame. For a split second, Sam's face was a mask of horror. His eyebrows were ruffled, his cheeks were pale, and his lips were twisted into a nightmarish grimace. He looked devastated, like a jubilant mouse that glances up from found cheese and encounters a swinging death blade.

Over the course of the next two seconds, Sam

gradually regained his composure. His eyebrows unwrinkled, his lips unfrowned. And three seconds after the blow, he even made a pathetic attempt to smile. Craig hit pause and zoomed in on Sam's contorted lips.

"Look at that," Eliza whispered. "He looks like a seizure victim."

"Let's turn it off," Craig said. "I can't watch it anymore."

He closed the window, and they sat for a moment in silence.

"Huh," Craig said. "That was March 23, 2011."

"So that's the date...?"

Craig nodded. "That's when their prayers came in."

There were eleven more meetings between Sam and Laura, ranging in length from two to twenty-three minutes.

"Do we need to watch them all?" Eliza asked.

Craig nodded and dutifully scrolled through the clips. They were painful to witness. The encounters always started positively—a chance meeting, a joyous hug, an animated discussion of recent television. But Sam always killed the momentum by asking Laura about her boyfriend.

"How's Cliff?" he'd blurt out, an extremely forced smile on his face.

"He's good!" she'd answer awkwardly.

And talk would quickly cease.

"Who's this Cliff guy?" Eliza asked.

"Let's check."

Craig popped up Laura's Romantic History—it was brief—and quickly found the boyfriend: Cliff Davenport, an experimental painter at Columbia University.

"Should we run ComCheck?" Eliza asked.

"Why not?"

Craig opened a window, entered the names, and waited for the results to tabulate.

Compatibility Check
Laura Potts/Cliff Davenport
Score: 28

Craig stared at the number in shock. With the exception of some prison relationships, it was the worst long-term pairing he'd ever seen. Laura and Cliff were incompatible on almost every level.

They were repulsed by the smell of each other's shampoo. They had completely different tastes in baby names. Laura was allergic to the only dish that Cliff knew how to cook. Their knuckles were positioned in such a way that it was uncomfortable for them to hold hands. Their families had never met, but if they did, they wouldn't get along.

Neither of them liked dark meat, so if they were to roast a chicken, half the carcass would be wasted. Their immune systems were structured in such a way that if one of them got sick, the other would automatically catch the illness. They had drastically different tastes in books and film and even people. They disagreed on how to pronounce "gyro."

There was only one positive aspect of their relationship: physical compatibility. Cliff and Laura scored a 97 on Sex—an extremely impressive statistic. They found each other's pheromones intoxicating. Their genitals were proportioned *and* positioned to provide each other with maximum pleasure. Their orgasms were unusually intense and almost always simultaneous.

"Are they still dating?" Eliza asked.

"I'm afraid to find out."

Craig logged out of the Server and scanned Laura's present-day apartment, a walk-up on Forsyth and Stanton.

"I don't see any evidence of a male presence," he said, eyeing the pink bedspread. "Let me count the toothbrushes in the bathroom."

He zoomed in on the human's sink. A lone yellow toothbrush lay behind the faucet.

"That's a good sign," he said. "I'll check her bureau for male underwear."

"There's got to be a faster way to do this," Eliza complained.

"Like what?"

"I don't know. Can't you just check Facebook?"

Craig's face reddened. "Good call."

He looked up Laura's account and smiled with relief.

Relationship Status: Single.

"Great," Eliza said. "She's single. Try Sam."

Craig typed in the human's name, but no profile came up.

"Guess he doesn't have an account."

"Geez. How antisocial can you get?"

"Let's watch him for a bit," Craig suggested. "If he's got a girlfriend, we'll find out about it soon enough."

He opened Omnex, typed in "Sam Katz," and hit enter. The computer located the human instantly, zooming in on the living room of his ground-floor apartment. Sam was sprawled on a futon, watching a show called *Bizarre Bodies* on Discovery Health.

"He's lost more hair," Craig noted.

"Yeah," Eliza said. "And gained at least fifteen pounds."

A buzzer sounded in Sam's apartment, and the human scrambled to his feet.

"Someone's coming," Eliza said. "Maybe it's a girlfriend."

"Maybe."

He turned up the volume, and the Angels anxiously leaned forward.

EARTH—THIRTY DAYS UNTIL DOOMSDAY

Sam Katz was about to open the door when he realized that he wasn't wearing any pants. He stood in the hallway for a moment, weighing his options. There were pants in his bedroom, but that was far away—and the buzzer had already rung twice. What was ruder, answering the door in your underwear or making someone wait? He was about to make a mad dash to his bedroom when the buzzer rang a third time, a long, insistent drone. He reluctantly opened the door.

A tall, mustachioed Indian man holding a red delivery bag stared down at him.

"Hey, Raj," Sam said, handing him a large clump of bills. "How's it going?"

"Where are your pants?" Raj demanded.

Sam forced a smile. "Sorry, Raj—I just came out of the shower and I didn't have time to put them on."

Raj folded his arms. "You did not just shower. You have not bathed all day. Admit this."

Sam chuckled evasively. "How's everything? How's Rubaina?"

"Do not change subject."

Raj leaned forward and continued in a whisper. "We are worried about you, Sam. Not just me. Everyone at Bombay Palace is worried."

He held up his delivery bag. "It is too much food for one man. Chicken vindaloo, lamb tandoori, Grand Sultan appetizer platter, soup, naan, mango lassi..." Raj shook his head. "Is too much."

"It's not—it's not just for me," Sam stammered. "I'm having a party...for friends."

Raj raised his eyebrows sarcastically. "Oh yes? Tell me then what are these friends' names?"

Sam averted his eyes. "Let's see, uh, John...Paul... George..."

Raj shook his head. "Those are Beatles. You are saying the names of famous Beatles."

Sam looked down at his feet. "It's all for me," he confessed.

"Sam?" Raj asked gently. "How long now I know you?"

Sam did the math in his head. He'd been ordering from Bombay Palace since freshman year of college.

"About four years?" he guessed.

"Four years," Raj agreed. "And we are friends, yes? I give extra puri, deliver past ten?"

Sam nodded. "Sure, Raj. We're friends."

"Then here is my advice."

He leaned toward Sam, his eyes narrowing. "I think it is time you find a wife."

Sam laughed. "Raj, I'm only twenty-three."

"By that age I was married with two strong sons."

"I know, but things are different for me. I mean, your marriage with Rubaina was *arranged.*"

"It is true," Raj said. "I have been fortunate."

The two men stood for a moment in silence.

"I include extra puri," Raj said. "And the green sauce you love."

"Thanks, Raj. I appreciate it."

The men shook hands formally and Sam closed the door, clutching his grease-splotched bag. Lately he had begun to order food in such large quantities that restaurants packed multiple sets of cutlery, assuming his meal was for several people. But this time, when he dumped his dinner onto the counter, just a single plastic fork tumbled out. He searched for a knife and spoon—but there weren't any. Evidently he was such an animal in the eyes of the Bombay Palace staff that they didn't think him worthy of a complete set. The chef probably assumed that he sopped up the sauces with bread or just drank them out of the plastic containers like a beast.

Sam reflected that he was in danger of going an entire day without wearing pants. He walked into his bedroom and picked up his rumpled corduroys. He could put them on for dinner, he supposed, but they were so tight and unpleasant to wear. He tossed them on the floor and shrugged. It's not like anyone was watching.

"Well," Eliza said. "I think we can assume he's single."

"I think that's a safe bet," Craig said.

"What's he watching?"

Craig zoomed in on Sam's television. "*Bizarre Bodies.* It's a show about humans with physical oddities."

"He couldn't find anything better to watch?"

"Well, there's not much on. It's the weekend. Most humans are out socializing."

Eliza shook her head in disgust. "When's the last time he left the house?"

Craig hit –×50, and they watched Sam's weekend in rewind. He plucked pieces of tandoori out of his mouth, returned them to their containers, and quickly restuffed the delivery bag. He zipped over to the front door, handed the food to Raj, and took back his money.

"Can you go faster?"

Craig hit –×500, and the action sped up dramatically. Sam's apartment brightened, darkened, and brightened again as the sun bobbed up and down outside his window. In his kitchen, a moldy baguette shed its greenish spots, regained its shape, and returned to an edible condition. But through it all Sam remained on his futon, as motionless as a corpse. With the exception of a single trip to a Rite-Aid, he hadn't left the house in three days.

"He's only six blocks from Laura," Craig said. "That's less than half a mile."

"Why does that suddenly seem so far?"

Craig fast-forwarded back to the present moment and hit play. On the screen, Sam dropped a piece of naan onto his filthy hardwood floor. He paused, looked out the window to make sure no one was watching, and then popped it into his mouth.

"Ugh," Eliza groaned. "What a mess."

"I think you're being a little hard on him," Craig said. "He's obviously going through a rough time. But lots of people feel lost at that age. I mean, the guy's only twenty-three years old."

"You know who else was twenty-three? Alexander the Great when he conquered the known world."

"I don't think that's a fair comparison."

"Why not? They're the same species, same gender, same age. They even look sort of alike."

Eliza grabbed Craig's mouse and opened the Server. A search box popped up, and she typed in "Alexander the Great—23 years old." The Macedonian conqueror appeared on the screen, sword in hand. A hundred captured slaves wept fearfully at his feet.

"I don't understand what this is supposed to prove," Craig said.

Eliza opened a window of Sam in present-day Manhattan and placed it alongside the twenty-three-year-old Alexander. They did look pretty similar. They were about the same height, five-seven or five-eight, and stockily built. Alexander was a touch more muscular, particularly in the shoulders. Sam had straighter teeth. Neither of them was particularly attractive.

Eliza and Craig sat quietly in front of the computer, silently comparing the two twenty-three-year-olds.

On the left side of the screen, Alexander pointed randomly at slaves, casually deciding which ones should die.

On the right side of the screen, Sam surfed the Web, in an obvious search for pornography.

"Okay," Craig said. "So Sam isn't as confident as Alexander. Who cares? Even if he's a total coward, things can still work out for him."

"How?"

"Well, it's 2012. Men don't have to make the first move. We still haven't seen Laura in the present day. Maybe she's less..."

"Pathetic."

"I was going to say 'reserved.' But yeah."

He located Laura's apartment and zoomed in.

"Let's see what we can find out."

EARTH—THIRTY DAYS UNTIL DOOMSDAY

Laura Potts sat in her darkened apartment watching *Bizarre Bodies.* She'd promised herself at 7 p.m. that she would watch only two episodes: "World's Fattest Man" and "The Wolf Family." Then she would put on her clothes, go to a bar, and socialize like a normal human being. But that was hours ago. She'd since sat through "Tumor Lady," "Conjoined at the Face," and an encore presentation of "Tumor Lady." It was 1:20 a.m. Technically, the night was already over.

Laura had turned twenty-three recently, and both of her older sisters had sent birthday cards. She'd displayed them on top of her television: a sparkly one from Katrina and a lengthy one from Dianne.

Growing up, Katrina had always been the "pretty one" and Dianne had always been the "smart one." Laura wasn't particularly pretty or smart, but her parents were desperate to give her some kind of identity. When she was nine, they bought her gymnastics lessons, thinking she might turn out to be the "athletic one." But she couldn't do even a single pull-up. When she turned ten, they bought her a monogrammed Bible, hoping she could at least become the "religious one." But she never got around to reading it. One day, at the age of twelve, she took some Polaroids of a tree out of boredom. From this random occurrence, her parents concluded that she was the "artistic one." They bought her an expensive camera, and she dutifully began to take pictures.

She went to NYU, majored in visual studies, and completed a thesis of abstract nature studies. She worked extremely hard. And by the time she graduated from college, she had discovered two major truths about photography: one, she didn't really like it; and two, she wasn't very good at it.

Now she was out of school and totally lost, barely surviving in a kitchenless apartment on the Lower East Side. Her only source of income was a job she'd found on Craigslist. Jack's Dawgs, a chain of downtown hot dog stands, had received straight Ds in a recent health inspection. So the owner, Jack Potenzone, was paying Laura to improve the chain's public image. Each day she went online and posted a hundred positive comments on food sites, using fictitious screen names.

"I don't know how Jack's Dawgs got such a bad rap," read a typical review. "Their stores are spotless, welcoming, and there are no rats."

Her boss had instructed her to insert the phrase "there are no rats" in every single one of her posts. "That way," he explained, "people will think we don't have rats."

Laura warned him that the constant use of the phrase might look suspicious. But Jack was adamant on the subject, and she didn't see any point in arguing. The job paid $250 a week and she was desperate for the income. In the brief time since college, she'd already amassed over $8,000 in credit card debt. She knew she should move back home, but she was afraid to face her parents. She was afraid to face anyone. With the exception of her daily coffee run to Dunkin Donuts, she rarely left her apartment.

The only people Laura spoke to were strangers who called her by accident. She'd gotten a new iPhone three weeks ago and her number was one digit off from the 101.1 FM sweepstakes line. She got about thirty misdials a day.

"Am I the hundred and first caller?" they all demanded. "Did I win?"

The first few times it happened, Laura apologized and explained that they'd dialed the wrong number—that she was a person, not a radio station. But the people always got so angry when she told them—cursing and arguing—that it made her depressed. Now when people asked if they had won, she usually just said yes.

She never knew what the contests were promising, so when people asked what prize they'd won, she'd make something up on the spot. So far this week, she'd given away ten tickets to the Super Bowl, four trips to Aruba, and a dinner with Pierce Brosnan. One time, when she was a little drunk, she gave a man a million dollars.

"Am I the hundred and first caller?" he'd shouted. "Tell me I'm the hundred and first caller!" It was 3 a.m. on a Wednesday, and he had been calling for forty minutes straight.

"Not only are you the hundred and first caller," she told him, "but you just won a million dollars."

"Un-fucking-believable!" he screamed. "I'm going to quit my job right now."

She felt a little guilty about that one.

Laura noticed that the callers never asked for any details. They never inquired about when their prize was going to arrive in the mail or where they should go to pick it up. She once told a stoned teenager that he was going to be launched into outer space. He didn't ask her when it was going to happen or how. He just sighed with relief, like he had been expecting to win a free space trip for some time.

"That'll show them," he said.

Recently she'd given a man free tickets to see Bruce Springsteen and he'd gotten mad at her.

"What's wrong?" Laura asked. "They're good seats."

"Nothing. It's just, I'm not the world's biggest Springsteen fan, all right?"

Since then she'd always made sure to ask callers what kind of prize they wanted. That way, she could give them something that would make them happy.

Laura felt bad about lying to people, but she found the calls strangely exhilarating. When she left her apartment, she had trouble ordering a cup of coffee. But when she talked to strangers on the phone, her voice came out loud and clear. She knew it was ridiculous, but giving away fake prizes was the highlight of her day.

She signed onto Facebook and searched idly for half-forgotten friends. A boy from her middle school who once set a Dumpster on fire was working as an insurance actuary in Hartford. Her bunkmate from Camp Wannago was gigantically pregnant. The bully from high school had shaved his whole head and was studying to be a Buddhist priest.

She typed in "Sam Katz." Nothing came up. She wondered if he was still in New York City and what had happened to him. She thought about sending him an e-mail, but she wasn't sure what to say.

On the television screen, two conjoined toddlers were feeding each other pieces of hamburger meat. The twins shared a laugh, and Laura felt an unmistakable stab of jealousy. It would be nice to always have someone by your side, someone to push hamburger into your face and make you smile.

It was nearly 2 a.m.

She took out her cell phone and held it in her hand, wondering if someone else would call.

"Good God," Eliza said. "They're both freaks!"

"This is worrisome," Craig agreed.

"'*Worrisome?*' They're a couple of shut-ins! How are we supposed to unite them if they won't even leave their apartments?"

She closed her eyes and massaged her temples. "We should've picked a different prayer."

Craig rose to his feet. "Maybe it's not too late."

"You want to give up *already?*" God laughed. "It's only been two days!"

"I'm not giving up," Craig said. "I just wanted to see if it would be possible to maybe switch to a different prayer? Like this one."

He slid a piece of paper across the desk. "It's about saving a hamster."

God leaned back in his chair and grinned.

"You know, in the restaurant business, we have a saying: 'You can't switch a customer's entrée, even if it comes out oversalted.' "

Craig stared blankly at his boss. He was pretty sure that wasn't a real restaurant saying.

"My point is," God continued, "just because you're losing doesn't mean you can change the rules of the game. You said you'd call your shot—and you called it. If you really care about saving this little planet, you'll make these two losers hook up."

Craig rubbed the bridge of his nose.

"How much time do I have?"

"I don't remember," God said. "But don't worry—I've got someone keeping track for me."

He flipped on his TV. On the screen the prophet Raoul was running around in a Walmart parking lot, screaming at shoppers. He wore nothing but a Speedo, and he held a giant cardboard sign over his head.

"The World Will End in 2012," it read. "Twenty-eight Days Until Doomsday."

"Well, there you have it," God said. "Guess you'd better get back to work."

Craig trudged out of God's office, past Vince's desk.

"Who's the hack now?" the Archangel muttered.

Craig turned toward him, confused. "I'm sorry—what?"

Vince reached for a nearby martini glass and raised it over his head in a sarcastic toast. Craig realized, with some concern, that the Archangel was intensely drunk.

"You always thought you were so clever," Vince said, slurring his words, "with your Gusts chart and your rainbows and your cutesy little snow days..."

He leaned toward Craig and continued in a whisper, "But now that the stakes are high—now that the pressure's on? You're lost. You're helpless."

He grinned. "You're *fucked.*"

Craig figured it was a good time to leave. He was about to turn his back on Vince when the Archangel pointed aggressively at his face.

"You know what's funny?" he said. "When the world explodes, all of your work will be erased forever. Those humans, the ones that come up here, they won't remember anything you did for them. It'll be like you never existed."

Craig knew there was no point in reasoning with Vince, but he couldn't help but take the bait.

"*I'll* still remember all the stuff I did," he said. He'd meant to sound defiant, but his voice came out squeaky and childlike.

Vince plowed ahead, obviously sensing his advantage. "Of course, you'll always have your memories. You can even hang your Angel of the Month plaques on your wall in a nice little row. But one day you're going to wake up and realize that in the grand scheme of things, all your work is completely insignificant."

Craig's lips began to quiver, and it looked to Vince

as if he might cry. But instead the Angel let loose a strange, high-pitched laugh.

"You think I don't know that?" Craig said. "You think I don't know that my work is insignificant? I've known that since day one! Last year I spent five months helping a woman win a tomato-planting contest—and then she forgot to enter! Every time I catch a kid a fish, his dad throws it back. I know I have no power—none of us has any power! I know none of it matters—but it matters to *me.* What the hell matters to you?"

Vince shifted awkwardly in his seat; he'd never heard Craig yell before.

"I'd love to talk more," Craig said. "But I've got work to do."

"Are you okay?" Eliza asked Craig. "You're sweating like crazy."

"I'm fine," he said, forcing a smile. "Let's just get started, all right?"

He heaped a pile of notes onto his desk. "I've arranged Chance Encounters before," he told her. "It's hard—but not impossible."

He flipped through his research. "Laura goes to Dunkin Donuts every day, usually around eleven. Sam takes the F train to work each day at nine-thirty. Maybe we could delay him somehow and alter his route? It would take some serious troubleshooting, but I'm sure we could get the humans to cross paths."

"And then what?"

Craig shrugged. "They start talking, sparks fly...romance follows?"

Eliza shook her head. "I don't know."

"What? What's wrong?"

"Even if your coding works—even if we can get the humans into the *exact same* spot at the *exact same* time—I think we still might be in trouble."

"What do you mean?"

Eliza paused, searching for a polite way to phrase her opinion. Eventually, she gave up.

"He's gotten crazy fat," she said.

Craig absentmindedly pinched his own love handles. "Sam's only fifteen pounds overweight," he said. "Twenty at most. It's not like he's obese or anything."

"Granted. But think of it from her perspective."

She opened up a clip of the humans' last meeting. "The last time she saw him, he looked like this." She pointed at Sam's relatively svelte 2011 physique.

"Now she's going to see him again and—boom! He's gonna look like this." She popped up a picture of Sam's current state. "It's *drastic.*"

Craig winced. Eliza's bar for male attractiveness was disturbingly high.

"He doesn't look terrible," Craig said. "He's just a little fat."

"He's a *lot* fat."

"It's not his fault. I mean, he's clearly going through

some kind of depression. Lots of people eat poorly when they're feeling down."

"I'm not blaming him. I'm just saying we need to do something."

She zoomed in on Sam's torso.

"If Laura runs into him on the street, she's not going to think, 'Oh, great, here's the guy I used to have a crush on.' The only thought in her brain is going to be 'Wow, how'd this happen? How'd he get like this?' I'm sorry, but that's just my opinion—as both an Angel and a woman."

Craig threw his hands up in frustration. "I don't know what to tell you. We can't just burn his fat off. It goes against the laws of thermodynamics."

"Can we change the way he dresses? So the weight gain is less pronounced?"

"He's got free will, Eliza. If he wants to wear khakis and a T-shirt, there's nothing we can do to stop him."

"Well, we've got to think of something."

The Angels sat in silence, plotting their next move.

EARTH—TWENTY-SEVEN DAYS UNTIL DOOMSDAY

Sam was walking to the F train when he encountered a harsh gust of wind. The blast of air was so intense he had to stop in midstride and shield his face with his hands. A swirl of airborne garbage engulfed him—plastic bags, cigarette butts, and lotto tickets.

"Jesus *Christ,*" he muttered to himself.

The draft eventually subsided, but one piece of trash remained stubbornly stuck to his coat—a small pink flyer. He plucked it off his chest and idly began to read it.

Join Crunch Fitness today! Full-service gym. Sign up now for a free one-month trial.

He glanced at the flyer for a moment, reflecting that the gym was just a block or so from his apartment.

"What a coincidence," he mumbled.

He folded the flyer a few times and then flicked it into a nearby garbage can.

Craig and Eliza sighed. It had taken them four hours to locate the flyer, blow it across the sidewalk, and successfully glide it onto Sam's body. But still the human had failed to take the hint.

"I really thought that would work," Eliza said. "I mean, how often does a gym coupon fly into your face? It's not like we were being subtle."

"It's hard to give the humans signs," Craig told her. "Ninety-nine times out of a hundred, they miss them. It doesn't matter how blunt you are."

"Really?"

Craig nodded. "They're just not a perceptive species.

Remember Archduke Ferdinand? The guy they shot to start World War One? Angels sent him fifty omens on the morning of his assassination to try to warn him. He ignored them all."

"Seriously? What kind of omens?"

Craig closed his eyes and listed a few from memory. There was the crow that landed on the archduke's windowsill, cawing aggressively in his face. There was the black cat that wandered past his doorway when he was preparing to leave his house. There was his gate's refusal to open. His car's refusal to start. The chill in the air, the foreboding gray sky, the terrible howling of the wind.

"You'd think he'd put two and two together," Craig said. "And call in sick."

Eliza squinted at the computer. Sam was heading uptown on the F train, a package of cherry Pop-Tarts in his hands.

"Even if he joins a gym," she said, "it won't really make much of a difference. I mean, we only have twenty-seven days to work with. It's not enough time for him to get in shape."

Craig swiveled toward Eliza. "Are you sure it matters how he looks?" he said.

"What do you mean?"

"Isn't love about more than physical appearances? I mean, these people are made for each other—their souls are a perfect match. Isn't that enough?"

The Angels sat for a moment in silence.

"He's still got to lose weight," Eliza said.

"Yeah," Craig murmured, sadly. "He looks like garbage."

He typed a new code into his computer.

"Don't worry," he told her. "I've got a backup plan."

Craig, like most Angels, was a master of self-delusion.

When he jammed a patrolman's radar gun to protect people from speeding tickets, he ignored the cop's quota and the grief he would get back at the station. When he helped a group of Boy Scouts start a campfire, he tried not to think about the carcinogenic properties of roasted marshmallows.

Craig spent twenty minutes a day crashing old people's computers to prevent them from sending their credit card numbers to Nigerian scam artists. But he never thought about the scam artists themselves and the money and joy he was costing them.

He was ecstatic when he helped St. Mary's School for the Blind win its first-ever middle school wrestling match. But the victory dealt a major psychological blow to their sighted opponents, one of whom had lost to a blind child in front of his parents. Was it still a miracle if someone had to suffer?

Craig was usually able to justify his actions with a cost-benefit analysis. As long as a miracle's "good" outweighed its "bad," he considered himself in the right.

Surgeons had to make incisions; firemen had to smash doors. It was all part of the game.

Still, he was finding it difficult to justify a salmonella attack.

"Okay," he said, his fingers fluttering over his keyboard. "That's the Bombay Palace freezer...and that's the vat where they keep the green sauce. It's already crawling with bacteria. All I have to do is knock out the freezer's power supply. It'll create enough warmth for the microbes to replicate and turn the sauce into poison."

He looked over at Eliza. "Are you absolutely sure that this is necessary?"

She nodded. "It's for the best."

EARTH—TWENTY-FIVE DAYS UNTIL DOOMSDAY

"This is first time all day you put on pants," Raj said. "You were naked until the moment I arrive."

"That's not true," Sam lied.

"Yes. You heard buzzer and put on pants, but before that you spend day naked. Admit this."

Sam looked down at his sockless feet.

"Okay," he admitted. "You're right."

"You need to get out of slump," Raj told him.

"I know."

"Everything happens for a reason. If life is hard, you must take it by the horns."

"I *know*. Okay? I know!"

Raj took a step back, surprised by Sam's unusual eruption.

"I'm sorry," he said. "It is because I care about you, that I say these things."

Sam sighed. "I know, Raj. I didn't mean to yell."

They stood for a moment in silence.

"I give extra puri," Raj said. "And the green sauce you love."

"Thanks, Raj. You're the best."

Sam tipped him generously and made his way back to the couch. It took him a few bites to realize that his food tasted a bit strange. Had they hired a new chef? He dipped his spoon into the green sauce and sipped it. It wasn't bad, he reflected—just different. He dumped the container onto his rice and finished his meal.

Twelve hours later, Sam lay in a fetal position on his bathroom floor, shivering. He groped for his cell phone and dialed up his office.

"I think it's food poisoning," he told a secretary. "Are you guys going to be all right without me?"

The secretary laughed. "Yeah, I think we'll manage."

Sam worked for a company called Chapman Consulting. He didn't have any particular interest in consulting, but of the two hundred résumés he sent out senior year, it was the only place that had offered him a job. He'd been extremely frightened to start work; he knew nothing about finance and was terrified he'd be exposed as a fraud. But so far nobody had noticed his ineptitude.

His boss was a friendly alcoholic named Mr. Dougan who wore the same pin-striped suit every day. He explained to Sam on his very first day of work that Chapman Consulting was something called a tax dodge. The financial specifics were over Sam's head, but basically a billionaire named Mr. Chapman had founded the company in the 1980s to hide some of his money from the government. Chapman Consulting never actually "did" anything. The company was purely for show: a physical space that nosy IRS agents could visit.

Mr. Dougan had been given his position as a reward for covering up some of Mr. Chapman's investment crimes. He arrived at the office each morning at eight and began to drink immediately.

Chapman Consulting occupied all three floors of a stunning midtown brownstone. There were about a dozen employees, women mostly, spread out all over the building. Since the company had no real business, they spent their days playing solitaire on their computers. When one of them won a game, her computer emitted a celebratory beep. Other than these beeps, the office was completely silent.

Sam's hours were nine to five. As soon as he arrived, Mr. Dougan called him into his office and ordered him to close the door. He then instructed him in a quiet voice to search through all the couch cushions in the building, collect all of the loose change he could find, and bring it back. This task usually took about thirty minutes. When Sam returned with the change, his boss had him divide the coins into two piles. He then dispatched him to Empire Bodega across the street with instructions to spend 50 percent of the change on beer and the other 50 percent on lottery tickets. When Sam returned with the purchases, Mr. Dougan hustled him back into his office, closed the door, and carefully divided the beers between them. When they were finished drinking them all, they took turns scratching off the lottery tickets. If any of the tickets were winners, Dougan immediately sent Sam back to the bodega with the same instructions as before. The cycle continued for as long as there was change to work with.

Sam liked his job. Before Chapman Consulting, he'd worked as a Starbucks barista—and he was much better at this one. He had a good eye for finding coins, and he never made a mistake dividing them. Even better, his boss really seemed to like him.

"You're doing a great job," Mr. Dougan often whispered to him when he came back with the beer and the tickets. "Close the door and drink your beers."

Sam felt a real fondness for his boss and hated to disappoint him. On days when the couches held little or no loose change, he supplemented his findings with coins from his own pockets. He felt bad about calling in sick and leaving Mr. Dougan on his own. But there was nothing he could do; he was too ill to stand. He'd spent the last eight hours within an arm's reach of the toilet bowl. He wasn't sure how it had happened, but he was completely naked. His bathroom looked like a crime scene.

It occurred to Sam that if he died, it would be several days before somebody found him. All his friends from college had scattered across the country after graduation. And he wasn't really in touch with his parents. They'd gotten divorced during his freshman year, and by his sophomore year, they had both remarried. They had started new families with shocking speed—his mother in California, his father in Texas. In just five years, he'd gone from being an only child to the oldest of eight. He had two half sisters (so far) and five stepsiblings. Sometimes, when talking to his folks on the holidays, he confused one parent's children with the other's.

Sam had planned to move back home after graduation, at least for a few months. But he wasn't sure what "home" meant anymore. His childhood house, his mother once casually mentioned, had been bulldozed. And while he knew he was welcome to visit either parent, neither had a bedroom waiting for him.

He gazed at his phone and noted with shock that it was almost 7 p.m. It was looking to be another no-pants day. He knew he should drink some water, but he didn't have the strength to stand. His daydreams, he noticed, were increasingly hallucinatory. He kept seeing faces in the bathroom tiles, and the toilet had begun to remind him of Raj—a towering, upright presence, glaring down at him.

"Take life by the horns," he heard it say. "Get out of the slump."

"How?" he whispered.

"Take life by the horns," Raj repeated.

Sam wiped the sweat from his brow. "Why did you poison me?"

"Everything happens for a reason," Raj said.

Sam closed his eyes, drifting gratefully into unconsciousness.

"I'm starting to get worried about him," Craig said. "He hasn't eaten anything in three days."

Eliza glanced at the screen. Sam had managed to crawl from his bathroom floor to his couch, but he was still in rough shape. His eyes were bloodshot, his cheeks a ghastly white. He'd attempted, at some point, to put on clothes. But he'd quickly abandoned the plan and was still naked except for a pair of mismatched socks. The television flashed in the darkness. A plastic bucket stood grimly by his side.

"Let it ride a little longer," Eliza said.

"Seriously?"

"It's working."

She zoomed in on Sam's pallid face. "See—he's already lost the double chin."

Craig raised his eyebrows. He had to admit: Sam was starting to look less doughy.

"Let's do another five days," Eliza suggested.

"*Four* more," Craig compromised. "We don't want him to die."

"Okay, okay. Four more days, starting now."

She stuck out her hand and Craig shook it.

EARTH—EIGHTEEN DAYS UNTIL DOOMSDAY

Sam tried to call in sick, but nobody at the office would pick up. It took him a few more tries to figure out why: it was Saturday. He'd lost seven days—an entire week of his life.

The strange thing, he realized, was that he didn't blame Bombay Palace. He knew it was their food that had poisoned him. But his love for the restaurant was so intense and pure he couldn't bear to find any fault with it. If anything, he felt guilty. Bombay Palace was not a popular restaurant, and Sam represented a sizable portion of its income. He was such a valued customer that Raj occasionally consulted with him before making changes to the menu. He hoped his seven-day absence hadn't caused too much damage to their business.

On Sunday morning he finally felt well enough to eat—and he immediately placed an order.

"Just one mulligatawny soup?" Raj asked over the phone. "That's it?"

Sam deliberated. He was extremely hungry, but he knew he should start off slow. There was only so much his recovering body could handle.

"Yes, thanks," he said. "Just the soup."

There was a long pause on the other end.

"Sam," Raj murmured. "I notice you do not order all week. What is the reason for this?"

Sam thought about telling Raj the truth, that his last delivery had badly sickened him. But he didn't want to make him feel guilty.

"I was on vacation," he lied. "You know, visiting family?"

"That is not true," Raj said. "You were ill from our food. Admit this."

"Jesus," Sam said. "How'd you know?"

"Because you ate the green sauce."

He took a deep breath and continued in a low tone. "Sam...I must confess to you. Last week many people who ate our green sauce...they had bad problems. Your sickness...it was our fault."

"It's okay, Raj. I don't blame you."

"You must. You are angry at me. Admit this."

Sam laughed. "I'm not mad—I swear! I mean, when you look at the amount of food I've ordered from you guys, it's amazing I've only been poisoned once. That's a pretty good percentage."

"Yes, well, I feel very bad," Raj said. "And so... the next three meals are free."

"You don't have to do that."

"Please. I have thought about this. I knew you were sick, because you stop ordering. And so I talk to Rubaina, and I say to her, 'I have sickened this man. What do I do?' I talk to her, and we decide I will bring the next three meals to you for free and no tip."

"Raj, really, you don't have to—"

"Yes," he interrupted. "Yes, I do! Please let me. I have bad sleep. I feel so bad... so bad to hurt my friend."

Sam started to respond, but his voice caught in his throat. He realized with shock that he was about to cry.

"Hello?" Raj asked. "Sam?"

Sam wiped his eyes. "That's really nice of you. Thanks, Raj."

"I will bring extra puri," he said. "And the *red* sauce this time."

Raj was at the door within ten minutes. They completed their customary handshake, and Raj handed Sam his food. The bag was oddly heavy, and when Sam peeked inside he noticed it contained extra soup. In addition to the mulligatawny he had ordered, there were three glass thermoses filled to the brim with pinkish broth.

"Is special soup not on menu," Raj explained. "Rubaina makes it for me when I am ill."

Sam noticed for the first time that Raj's cheeks were unusually gaunt.

"Oh, no," he said. "Don't tell me you were sick too?"

"Everyone was sick," Raj whispered. "It was like a plague at Bombay Palace."

His eyes took on a haunted look as he told the horrible tale.

"First the waiters get sick. Then the busboy. Then everybody. Our chef—Raveesh—he had an attack in the middle of the restaurant. He could not make it to the staff toilet. There was no time. So he ran into the customer toilet, right in front of everybody. Can you imagine how that is for business? There are customers sitting at tables and they see the chef, wearing his chef's hat, run into bathroom and begin to scream. Really scream—like he is a dying man. Many customers get up and leave."

"That sounds awful."

"Yes. I ask myself, 'Why are we being punished? What crime have we committed to deserve such misfortune?'"

He leaned in close and continued in a whisper, "But the universe is mysterious. We can never know its plan."

Sam nodded awkwardly. "I guess that's true."

He thanked Raj again for the soups and promised to return the glass thermoses when he was done.

"If missing," Raj warned him, "my wife will become crazy."

"I understand," Sam said.

They said their good-byes and, for the first time ever, clumsily attempted an embrace.

Sam closed the door and stared excitedly at the bag. It had been seven days since his last real meal, and he had no idea what his body could handle. But he was feeling unusually confident. He was ready to take a risk.

He poured Rubaina's soup into a bowl and tentatively dipped his spoon into the broth. It smelled like mulligatawny, but it had a completely different consistency. It was chunkier, more substantial. He took a deep breath, closed his eyes, and took a tiny sip. In an instant, the drop of soup seemed to ricochet all over his mouth, coating his tongue with flavor. There was a stab of spiciness in the back of his throat, and a rush of endorphins flooded his bloodstream. He leaned back on the couch, looked up at the ceiling, and laughed.

He stood up suddenly. It was time, he decided.

It was time to put on pants.

"He's on the move!"

Craig scrambled into Eliza's cubicle.

"He's just getting out of the shower now," he told her breathlessly. "He's got pants laid out. I think he's going to leave the apartment."

Eliza pumped her fist. They'd been preparing for this moment all week, scanning hundreds of pages of data, producing countless lines of code. And now, after seven straight days of monotonous research, it was finally time to put their plan into action. It was finally time to answer the humans' prayers.

"Okay," Craig said. "I'm initiating the sequence."

He extended an index finger and shakily dangled it over the enter key.

"What are you waiting for?" Eliza demanded.

"Just a little nervous," Craig admitted. "I've never done this kind of thing before."

Eliza glared at him. "I thought you said you'd arranged Chance Encounters!"

"Of course I have!" he said. "Just...never in New York City."

They zoomed in on the dense street grid of the Lower East Side, swirling with cars and people.

"Everything's in place. If we mess up, we don't get another shot."

"Just press the button," Eliza shouted. "Press it!"

Craig wiped a bead of sweat off his forehead and jabbed the button with his finger. There was nothing they could do but watch.

Craig was no stranger to troubleshooting. In his years at the Miracles Department, he'd designed thousands of miracles, some of them dizzyingly complex. But when it came to Chance Encounters, he was as nervous as anyone on the floor.

Chance Encounters (or CE's) were so hard to plan

that few Angels even attempted them. In order to get two humans to converge at the exact same spot at the exact same time, you had to manipulate hundreds of variables. It took creativity, timing, and a hellish amount of research. And if you screwed up even a single detail, all was lost.

Laura lived on Forsyth and Stanton; Sam on Delancey and Ludlow. They were barely six blocks from each other—but in New York City, six blocks might as well be six light-years. The humans were separated by 841 walls and more than 100,000 people.

The Angels batted around dozens of strategies before eventually settling on a game plan. Like most twenty-three-year-old humans, Sam and Laura couldn't function long without their iPhones. If their phones were broken, they'd have no choice but to leave their apartments and get them repaired. The Apple Store on Allen and Rivington was located halfway between Sam's and Laura's apartments. It was the perfect spot for a Chance Encounter.

When Craig pressed enter, it simultaneously crashed both humans' phones. Within five seconds, they were staring at their frozen screens, jabbing at them frantically and cursing under their breath. There was nothing they could do, they quickly realized; they'd have to pay a visit to the Apple Store.

Sam—who was already wearing pants—scooped up his ruined machine and headed straight out the door.

Laura, though, remained stubbornly on her couch. With Sam on the move, the Angels couldn't afford to let Laura procrastinate. Luckily, they'd developed a contingency plan, designed to force her out of her apartment. First they increased the pressure to her radiator, causing it to click abrasively. When that didn't get her to leave, they short-circuited her cable box, depriving her of television access. She stood up and cursed for a while, but ultimately sat back down. The Angels, growing desperate at this point, located the nearest infant—a three-month-old boy two floors above Laura's apartment—and increased the gas pressure in his stomach. The baby started shrieking, at greater and greater volumes. Eventually, Laura couldn't take it anymore. She threw on an overcoat, tossed her iPhone into her bag, and headed for the door.

By the time she left her apartment, Sam was just a hundred feet from the Apple Store. If the Angels didn't stall him, he'd be in and out by the time Laura arrived. They tried to delay him with a succession of "Don't Walk" signs. But that ploy wasn't buying them enough time. Eventually, they had no choice but to arrange a minor car accident between a taxicab and an elderly man's Honda Civic. Neither driver was hurt, but their screaming match provided a useful diversion. By the time Sam was finished watching them, four minutes had passed—and Laura was entering the store.

Sam was about to enter as well, when disaster struck.

"Help...I need somebody...help..."

A talented street performer had begun to play one of Sam's favorite Beatles songs. The Angels watched in horror as Sam turned his back on the Apple Store and headed over to watch the guitarist. He tossed a single into the musician's empty case and bobbed his head in time to the music.

"It's okay," Craig whispered to Eliza. "It's a short song."

The street performer finished "Help" and immediately transitioned into "Hey Jude." Craig smacked his desk with annoyance.

"Rain?" Eliza suggested.

Craig hurriedly typed in a code, and the sky opened up with a roar. The musician packed up his gear and fled for the closest subway tunnel. Sam hustled into the Apple Store, grateful for some shelter from the storm.

By the time he entered the shop, Laura was standing at the cash register. They didn't initially notice each other, so the Angels made Sam sneeze, over and over, until Laura finally caught sight of him.

"Oh my God...Sam?"

"Laura? What are you doing here?"

The two humans hugged. The Angels subtly dimmed the store's lights and short-circuited the radio, shifting the station from classic rock to smooth jazz.

"How's Cliff?"

"Oh, we broke up."

"Really? Wow, that's... that's too bad."

Craig maximized the window on his computer screen. Eliza's face was so close to the monitor she could feel her hair sizzle with static electricity.

"You look good," Laura said.

Sam blushed.

"So do you!"

The Angels high-fived.

"It's happening!" Craig cried. *"It's happening!"*

Eliza moved even closer to the screen.

"Come on," she whispered. *"Ask her out."*

"So," Sam said to Laura. "What are you doing..."

"Tonight!" Craig shouted at the screen. *"What are you doing tonight!"*

Sam cleared his throat. "What are you doing... at the Apple Store?"

The Angels cursed with frustration.

"Well, my phone broke... so... here I am."

Eliza slapped the side of the computer monitor. *"Ask him out! Don't wait for him to do it! Just go! Go!"*

Laura shifted her weight from foot to foot.

Sam feigned interest in a nearby iPad display.

Eliza pulled at her hair. *"Come on!"*

"Well, hey," Sam said, eventually. "It was nice running into you."

"You too," Laura said. "I guess... I'll see ya?"

"Yeah! Yeah. I'll see ya."

The humans shook hands awkwardly and parted

ways. Just before Laura left the store, she glanced over her shoulder at Sam. He turned around a second later—but by then she was already out the door.

Craig leaned back in his office chair and covered his face with his hands.

"I don't believe it. All that work...the car accident, the rainstorm, the salmonella—what the hell happened?"

"They blew it," Eliza whispered. "They fucking blew it."

She yanked the power cord out of the wall and sighed as the screen went black.

Part II

HEAVEN—SEVENTEEN DAYS UNTIL DOOMSDAY

GOD LAUGHED.

"An *extension?* Out of the question."

"Just an extra month!" Craig pleaded. "We're so close. We arranged a Chance Encounter recently—there was *definite* chemistry between the humans. If we could just get them together one more time—"

"They had a chance and they screwed it up," God said. "Why don't you just quit?"

Craig sighed. For the first time in weeks, the question seemed valid.

"Look," God said. "I'd love to help you out. But I can't just postpone the earth's destruction. The date's already on the calendar. If I change it now, it would be a scheduling nightmare."

"For who?"

"Well, Raoul, for starters."

God turned on his TV, and his prophet popped onto the screen. He was standing by the Dumpster of an A&P, draped in foil and screaming at cars as they passed. His cardboard sign read: "The World Will End on Oct 3rd."

"He's been telling everyone October third," God explained. "I can't just tell him to rewrite all his signs. It took him hours to draw them."

"Could you at least ask him?"

God hesitated. "Okay," he said. "I'll ask."

He waved at the screen until he got Raoul's attention.

"Hey, buddy!" God shouted. "How's it hanging?"

Raoul shrugged. "Low and lazy."

God laughed for a while.

"Listen, one of my Angels wants me to push back the destruction date. How hard would it be to change the date on your signs?"

Raoul's eyes widened. "On *all* of them?"

"I'm not saying you have to!" God assured him. "I just wanted to know how hard it would be."

"Pretty damn hard," Raoul replied tensely.

"Forget it, then," God said. "Sorry I interrupted! Keep up the good work."

Raoul picked up his sign and sprinted after a nearby SUV.

God grinned apologetically at Craig. "Guess that answers that!"

Craig peeked at God's desk calendar. In the October 3 square, he'd written a memo to himself: "Don't forget: destroy Earth (fire?)" In the October 4 square, he'd written, "Restaurant opens!" and drawn several smiley faces.

"It's so close," Craig said. "It's hard to believe."

"I know," God said. "Just think: in eighteen days, we'll be sitting at a corner table at Sola, eating delicious Asian fusion."

He leaned back in his chair, clasping his hands behind his head. "I can hardly wait."

Craig slunk down the hall, trying his best to avoid eye contact with Vince. He had almost made it to the elevators when the Archangel called out his name. Craig took a deep breath to steady himself and slowly turned around.

"What do you want, Vince?"

"I watched your CE on the Server. Pretty clever."

Craig nodded awkwardly, unsure if Vince was being sarcastic.

"How'd you get that baby to start crying like that? Were you running a migraine program?"

"Actually, it was just a simple gas code."

He recited it from memory, and Vince slowly repeated it back.

"What about those sneezes?" he asked. "How'd you cue them?"

"I directed some gusts into the human's nose hairs."

"Those must've been pretty narrow gusts."

"I used a wind current."

"Oh, right. Of course."

They were silent for a moment.

"You know what I would've done?" Vince said. "I would've knocked Sam into a display case. Broken his legs or something. That way the female would have had no choice but to stay with him for a bit—you know, at least until the ambulance came. Also, it would've scored him a *crazy* amount of sympathy points. She'd definitely go visit him in the hospital, maybe even start pushing him around in his wheelchair. Sooner or later they'd start fucking."

Craig nodded. "That might've worked."

"It was just an idea," Vince said, flicking his wrist to emphasize how little effort he'd spent on it. "I'll see you around."

Craig smiled, slightly startled. Since when did Vince start "seeing him around"?

"Yeah," he said, "I'll see you around, Vince."

* * *

Eliza took a bottle of bourbon out of her desk drawer. They were pathetic, these humans, so cowardly and dumb. She took a swig of whiskey and idly scanned the globe.

A teenage ballerina in Warsaw feigned an ankle injury, to get out of a frightening audition.

A tourist in Paris canceled her dinner reservation, because she feared the wait staff would mock her French.

A child in Florida refused to ride Space Mountain, even though he was well over the height limit.

Eliza searched for Sam and Laura. They were both engrossed in their newly mended iPhones, scrolling robotically through a series of random tweets. Eliza wondered if they were thinking about each other, if they were conscious of how badly they had screwed up.

She looked at her watch. It was only 3 p.m., but she was thinking about leaving the office. It wasn't like anyone would notice.

"Is that bourbon?" Craig asked, poking his head into her cubicle.

Eliza offered him the bottle. "Want some?"

He shook his head. It was the first time they'd spoken to each other since their Chance Encounter had ended in disaster. Their failure seemed to hang in the air. Its presence was so mortifying they couldn't even look at each other.

"What'd God say?" Eliza asked.

"He wouldn't give us an extension. He thinks we should just give up."

"Makes sense."

Craig surveyed the floor and saw that it was almost completely empty. Ever since God's memo, Angels had started leaving work earlier and earlier. Some had already begun to clear out their desks; the cubicles were littered with half-filled cardboard boxes.

"So," Craig said. "What are you going to do next? You know, after the office closes?"

Eliza shrugged. "I might get into shuffleboard," she said. "That seems like a fun game."

Craig nodded. "I've walked by those courts. They look nice."

"What about you?"

Craig thought for a second. "I guess I'll help God with that restaurant," he said. "Maybe it's not such a bad idea? I mean, chic decor, reasonable prices—I could see it catching on."

"Yeah. Totally."

They didn't speak for a couple of minutes. Eventually, their silence was interrupted by a beeping sound.

Craig glanced at Eliza's computer and forced a laugh.

"Huh," he said. "A Potential Miracle."

Eliza squinted at her screen. In Belgium an elderly woman and her grandson were scrambling up a hill, trying to catch the last bus home. The driver was approaching their stop, and if they didn't flag him down in time, they'd be stranded.

Craig and Eliza turned away from the screen, feigning nonchalance. Who cared about some random humans in Belgium? The entire world was about to explode. As the humans struggled onward, though, both Angels turned unconsciously toward the screen.

"Come on," Craig whispered under his breath. "Move it."

The elderly woman was almost at the top of the hill when she stopped to catch her breath. She clutched her grandson's arm for support and squinted anxiously at the bus. It was already slowing for their stop.

Craig and Eliza made eye contact—and immediately burst into action.

"We gotta stall the driver," Eliza said.

"A crash is too risky."

"Can we cut out the engine?"

Craig recited a code and Eliza typed it rapidly into the computer. The bus's motor overheated, forcing the driver to stop. And by the time he could restart his vehicle, the grandmother and grandson had inched their way to the top of the hill. The driver spotted them in his rearview mirror and thrust his doors wide open.

"Yes!" Eliza shouted.

Craig pumped his fist. "Boo-yah!"

The Angels looked down at their feet, embarrassed by their sudden outburst. After a few awkward seconds, Craig cleared his throat.

"I don't want to give up," he confessed.

Eliza beamed at him. "Me neither."

"Really?"

She nodded. *"Really."*

Craig was so relieved he started to laugh.

"Oh, that's great!" he said. "That's great!"

He clapped his hands excitedly. "You stay right there! I'll make the coffee."

He ran to the break room and brewed a ferociously strong pot. By the time he returned with it, Eliza was hunched over her keyboard.

"I was thinking," Craig said. "If we break their iPhones again, it wouldn't be hard to arrange a second Chance Encounter. All we'd have to do this time is..."

He noticed that the blood had drained from Eliza's face.

"What's wrong?"

Eliza clicked her mouse a few times, zooming in on Laura's tiny bathroom sink. A pair of toothbrushes rested behind the faucet—both of them recently used.

"He's at her house," she whispered.

"Who? *Sam?*"

"No," Eliza muttered. "Cliff."

EARTH—FIFTEEN DAYS UNTIL DOOMSDAY

"I'm going to start a revolution," Cliff said. "The mainstream galleries are trying to ignore me, but I'm going to have the last laugh."

Laura nodded absently. Cliff had been telling her about his revolution for several years.

"Sure, I could play by their rules," he went on. "Sell a bunch of paintings, make ten million dollars. It would be the easiest thing in the world. But where would the victory in that be?"

"Well, you'd have ten million dollars."

Cliff scoffed. "That's so like you."

Laura flushed. "What do you mean?"

"I'm sorry," he said, kissing her on the forehead. "You can't help it. It's your whole middle-class upbringing. You've been taught to buy into so much bullshit."

Laura averted her eyes. She always got embarrassed when Cliff brought up class. She wasn't entirely sure about his background, but she knew he was from a poor family. His father had been some kind of baker—pastries, she'd heard him say one time. He'd mentioned once that he didn't have any student loans, which meant he'd somehow earned himself a full Ivy League scholarship. That alone was more than anything she'd ever accomplished.

"My point," Cliff said, "is that the bourgeoisie is frightened of my work. And with good reason. It has the potential to turn their fragile little world upside down."

Laura wondered what it would feel like to be as confident as Cliff. She never felt lazier than when he rambled on about his projects. He was currently working on five abstract paintings, a performance art piece, two separate operas, and a screenplay based on *Finnegans Wake.* He hadn't technically started writing the screenplay, but he was in the "final planning stages," which Laura thought was still somewhat impressive.

She looked over and noticed that Cliff was still talking—something about Borges now. Laura sighed. She didn't particularly like him. Still, after so many months of isolation, it was a relief to hear another human voice, even one as loud as his. When he called her out of the blue, she pressed "ignore." But as the week went on, her loneliness mounted and she eventually called him back.

"We've just become a nation of consumers," Cliff was saying. "They should call it the United States of Halliburton. In the Almighty Dollar We Trust."

Laura thought about her bizarre run-in with Sam. It was such a crazy coincidence; she had just been thinking about him, and then—boom—there he was.

"What do you think?" Cliff asked.

Laura hesitated. She hadn't been paying attention.

"I think you're right," she said.

Cliff kissed her passionately. "You're the only one on this planet who gets me," he said. "It's a real miracle we found each other."

Eliza stared at the screen with dismay.

"How did this happen?"

"It's a nightmare," Craig agreed. "I've researched this guy extensively; he sucks."

The Angels watched with disgust as Cliff slid his hand down Laura's nude back.

"I'm sorry for ranting," he told her. *"It's just, when I think about my art, I get so fired up. It's like a flame inside my heart that won't stop burning."*

"Ugh!" Eliza said. "Does that line ever work?"

"I checked his Sexual History," Craig said. "It works seventy-seven percent of the time."

"What? Seriously?"

Craig nodded glumly. "His success rate is even higher when he tries it on women under twenty."

Eliza shook her head. "I don't believe you."

Craig opened the Server and pulled up some of Cliff's recent sexual conquests. He'd used the "art" line—or variations on it—on thirteen different females in the past six months. All but three had responded with sexual contact of some kind.

"How could women fall for that?" Eliza moaned. "It's so obviously bullshit!"

Craig scrolled through his research file. "He's also had success with 'I would die for my films' and 'Have you ever read Spinoza?' "

They forced themselves to watch some recent clips. Cliff always uttered the phrases in the same way, with a guttural delivery that bordered on a sob.

"He *is* good-looking," Eliza admitted. "I mean, if you forget every single thing about him."

Craig zoomed in on Cliff's face. His skin was clear and

tan, and a perfectly manicured beard adorned his chiseled jaw.

"How can Sam compete with that?" she lamented.

"Maybe he's got some good pickup lines too?"

"Let's check."

Craig typed in a quick search. According to the Server, Sam's most common phrases in sexual situations were "We don't have to if you don't want to," "I'm sorry," and "Please don't tell anyone."

"Holy moly," Eliza said. "What a fucking mess."

She turned away from the screen in disgust. "How did this Cliff moron get a scholarship to Columbia?"

"He didn't. In fact, for the school to let him in, his family had to promise the dean two gyms and a particle accelerator."

"I thought his family was in the pastry business?"

"They are. Cliff's dad is the majority shareholder for the Americo Pastries Company."

"Whoa. I guess that's why he's in no rush to sell art."

"He's not in any rush to *make* any, either. Every project he told Laura about is made up."

Craig accessed Cliff's hard drive and opened a document titled "Finnegans Wake Screenplay."

Eliza read the file out loud. "Open on: nothingness."

She squinted incredulously at the screen. "That's it?"

Craig nodded. "We need to get rid of this guy."

"How hard can it be? It's not like Laura's in love with him or anything."

"Still, as long as he's around, I doubt she'll make any moves for Sam."

"Maybe *he'll* make a move."

Eliza shook her head. "I've been following his progress. It's pretty bleak."

She opened a window and zoomed in on Sam's bedroom. He was hunched over his computer, drafting an e-mail to Laura.

"He's writing her a message!" Craig exclaimed. "That's promising!"

"Not really," Eliza said. "He's been writing it for two days. Look."

She clicked the rewind button, and the Angels watched as Sam's fingers fluttered over his laptop. With the exception of a few breaks for sleeping and eating, he'd been revising his e-mail to Laura for the last forty-eight hours.

"He's written six different versions," Eliza marveled. "And erased all of them."

"Why? How bad could they be?"

She pulled up the first one. "See for yourself."

Greetings, Laura,

It was such a delightful coincidence running into you yesterday morn. When I walked into the Apple Store, I never guessed I'd have such a surprise in "store" for me!

Sincerely,

Sam Katz

"Want to hear something crazy?" Eliza said. "That e-mail took him over an hour to write."

"And he ended up with a pun on the word 'store'?"

Eliza nodded. "The next one is even worse."

yo, lemme know if you wanna hang sometime—S

Craig squinted at the screen. "What the hell is *that?*"

"He's trying to look cool," Eliza explained. "He wants her to think that his life is so busy and exciting that he couldn't be bothered to write her a proper letter. You know, like he dashed the thing off in ten seconds."

"How long did it actually take him?"

"Nearly six hours."

"How is that *possible?*"

"He just kept second-guessing himself. It took him over an hour to commit to 'yo.' First it was 'hey,' then 'hi,' then 'wassup,' then back to 'hey.' For about twenty minutes, he was going to lead with *'howdy.'* Can you imagine?"

Craig did a quick mental inventory of all the e-mails he'd ever sent Eliza. Had they been too casual? Too studied? Had he ever used the word "howdy"? They'd spent the last two weeks practically living together—drinking coffee from each other's mugs, chewing on each other's pencils, nodding off on each other's shoulders. But the more time they spent together, the more panicked Craig became. He never saw Eliza outside of work—and unless a miracle happened, he would soon be out of a job. He was running out of time.

"Have some fucking *confidence,*" Eliza said.

Craig's body tensed with panic—until he realized she was talking to the screen.

"It's his last draft," she said. "A real heartbreaker."

Dear Laura,

It was so much fun running into you at the Apple Store! I've really missed hanging out with you. I know this is out of the blue, but I was wondering if you'd like to grab a drink sometime?

Sam

"What's wrong with that one?" Craig asked.

"Nothing. He rattled it off in twenty seconds and it's perfect."

"I thought you said it was heartbreaking."

"Yeah. Because he didn't send it."

She zoomed in on Sam, present-day. He was hunched over his laptop, his shoulders tensed, his forehead damp. He was beginning another draft.

The Angels watched as he typed the letter H, followed by O, W, and D. Eliza closed the window before he could complete the word.

"I wonder how Alexander the Great was with women," Eliza said.

She opened the Server and zoomed in on ancient Macedonia.

"I don't see why that's relevant," Craig said.

"I'm just curious."

On the screen, Alexander sat on his throne, idly sipping wine from a silver jug. A row of women stood before him, each one of a different ethnicity. A few weary soldiers knelt by Alex's feet, anxiously awaiting his command. Eliza clicked the translate icon so they could watch the clip with subtitles.

"These females are mine by right," the ruler said. *"For I am a living god."*

His men nodded fearfully. Alex scratched his chin and then pointed casually at one of the women, an Asian beauty with slender hips and large black eyes. When he snapped his fingers, she took off her clothes and gracefully spun in a circle.

"Your body pleases me," Alex said. *"I will soon impregnate you."*

Craig laughed. "Can you believe this guy?"

Eliza shrugged. "I think he's kind of sexy."

Craig knew it was crazy to envy a dead Macedonian, but he couldn't stop his face from flushing. He forced a laugh to mask his jealousy.

"What's sexy about him?"

Eliza shrugged. "There's just something about the way he carries himself."

He watched in pained silence as Eliza zoomed in on the tyrant's rugged face.

"My power mocks Zeus," Alexander was saying. *"And when he sees my feats he is afraid."*

He gestured at the row of women. *"I will impregnate all of you. One after the other. And you will give birth to a race of living gods."*

A little sigh escaped from Eliza's lips.

"Okay," Craig said. "This is a lot of fun. But can we maybe get back to Sam now?"

"Sure," Eliza said, clearing her throat. "Just a second..."

Craig watched with annoyance as she tagged the Alexander clip as a favorite. Eventually, she closed the Server and typed in a search for Sam.

"Looks like he's back to square one," she said, as the human reappeared on the screen. He'd erased his entire e-mail and was taking a break to play Minesweeper.

"I don't know what to do," Eliza whispered. "I feel completely powerless."

"Me too," Craig confessed.

He stared at the screen, his jaw clenched with frustration. For the first time ever, he fantasized about punishing the humans. It would be so easy. Just a few taps of the keys, and he could easily zap them with lightning, fling them out their windows, break their legs...

A strange thought suddenly occurred to him.

"Eliza," he said. "How would you feel if I brought someone else on board? You know, like, for reinforcements?"

Eliza laughed. "The only person who still comes by is Brian—and that's just to use the ice machine."

"Not Brian. I know someone *good*. Well—not 'good.' He's actually vaguely evil. But I think he might be able to help us."

"Someone I know?"

"You've met him. He used to work on seventeen, but now he works upstairs. With God."

Eliza's eyes widened. "You don't mean..."

Craig nodded. "Let's just ask him. I mean, honestly—what have we got to lose?"

Craig stood outside the executive boardroom, trying to work up the courage to knock. He could see Vince through a crack in the door, his arm stretched out to light God's cigar.

"Come on," the Archangel was saying. "Let's do one."

God shook his head, but he was already laughing a little.

"We shouldn't."

Vince shoved him playfully on the shoulder. "Come on. We haven't done one for a while."

God hesitated for a moment, but he couldn't conceal his excitement.

"Okay, fine!" he said, standing up. "But this is the last one for at least a month."

Vince and the other Archangels cheered. One of them handed God his remote control, while another turned on the enormous TV that was mounted on the wall of the boardroom.

God scrolled through the channels before eventually settling on a desert in Tanzania. A tired farmer was leading his horse over a hill. God stretched out his index finger and coyly circled the red button.

"Do it!" the Archangels shouted. "Do it!"

God pressed the button and the horse exploded. His owner screamed with fear as the carcass rained down on him in clumps.

God shook his head and laughed.

"I love spontaneous combustions," he said. "Did you see the look on that guy's face?" Tears were forming in his eyes. "Did you *see?*"

Vince was trying not to spit out his drink, but he lost the battle and sprayed scotch all over the table. "Everyone's going to think he made it up!"

A younger Archangel pounded his fist against the boardroom table. "Hey!" he said. "Let's make crop circles!"

God poured himself a drink. "Oh, what the heck," he said. "It's Friday."

Craig rapped lightly on the door, but no one seemed to hear him. He took a deep breath and walked into the room.

"Hey!" God shouted. "It's Sola's number-one investor! What can I do for you?"

Craig swallowed, suddenly conscious of everyone's eyes on him.

"I'd like to speak to Vince," he said, turning toward the Archangel. "If you've got a moment."

"What do you want?" Vince asked suspiciously.

Craig hesitated. "Your help."

"Let's walk and talk."

Craig nodded and followed Vince down the hall. There were no cubicles in the executive wing, he noticed. Just plush leather chairs, mahogany tables, and mounted animal heads of every shape and size. Within seconds Craig had spotted a rhinoceros, an elephant, and one other creature—the largest by far—with reddish-brown fur and giant snow-white tusks. When he tiptoed past the head, he realized it was a woolly mammoth.

A Japanese chef smiled at them from behind a cart. "Sashimi?"

Craig started to say no, but Vince interrupted him.

"Toro," he said, holding up two fingers.

The chef quickly handed them two black plates, heaped high with slabs of fish. The slices were bright orange and striped with thin white ribbons of fat. Craig took some chopsticks from the cart and tentatively tried a piece. It turned liquid in his mouth, coating his tongue with salty oil. He closed his eyes, shocked by its richness.

"Holy shit," he said. "How could it be so good?"

"Life's pretty sweet up here," Vince said. "It's a shame you're still stuck on seventeen."

"I like it on seventeen."

"Do they still have that old vending machine? With the Hostess cupcakes?"

"Yeah," Craig said, smiling. "I had one this morning."

"Those things taste like shit."

Vince poured himself a scotch from a nearby decanter and took a seat in a leather chair.

"So," he said grandly. "How can I help you?"

Craig updated the Archangel as quickly as he could, conscious that Vince's eyes kept wandering to a nearby clock.

"We're not making much progress," Craig said. "So I figured, maybe we should add someone to the team? You know, someone bold, who can think outside the box."

"You want me to recommend someone?"

"No," Craig said. "I want *you.*"

Vince crossed his arms.

"I'd love to help," he said. "But I've already got a lot of important projects on my plate."

"*Do* you?"

Vince paused. "No," he admitted. "Not really. This

week God has me designing menus. Every time I show him a mock-up he complains that it isn't 'fusion' enough." He sighed. "I'm starting to think he doesn't know what that word *means.*"

Craig nodded sympathetically.

"Do you ever miss the department?"

Vince snorted. "Of course not."

"Come on. You must've liked it better than what you're doing now. I mean, what's the point of climbing the ladder if you don't have any freedom?"

"Maybe he'll promote me again."

"To what? Partner? You know what happened to the last Archangel who asked for that."

Vince nodded. God had gotten so angry at the guy that he accused him of "pride" and forced him out of the company. It had been a real scene.

"I know it isn't perfect up here," Vince said. "But at least you get some recognition. On seventeen you're invisible."

"That's not true."

"Of course it's true. I used to work all day, every day, helping those moron humans with their tiny lives. No one ever noticed."

Craig shrugged. "I noticed."

Vince was silent for a while. When he finally spoke, his voice came out unusually faint. "You said I was a hack."

"I don't remember saying that."

"You *said* it."

"Well, I didn't mean it."

"Then why'd you say it?"

Craig grimaced, irritated by the conversation's turn.

"Because I was *jealous,*" he said. "Vince, if I had as much confidence as you, or even *half* as much..." He looked down at his lap. "My life would be a lot different."

When he looked up, he saw that Vince was blushing.

"Okay," the Archangel said. "I'm in."

"Really?"

Vince set down his drink and extended his hand. Craig exhaled with relief and pumped it wildly.

"Oh, this is great news!" he said. "And it's going to be fun, too! I promise!"

Vince and Eliza stared icily at each other from across the break table. After several long minutes of silence, Craig returned with the coffee.

"Two cups of joe," he said. "For my *two* partners!"

He handed them their coffee and grinned, trying to defuse their hostility.

"What'd I miss?" he asked nervously.

"Your colleague was just attacking my basketball miracle," Vince said. "You know, the universally beloved one."

"I wasn't attacking it," Eliza said. "I just asked if it was yours, because it seemed like your style. You know, melodramatic and ridiculous."

Craig sighed. Vince's basketball miracle was nearly five years old, but some Angels were still angry about it. It was one of the sloppiest miracles in company history. The event took place in western Pennsylvania. It was the last game of the season for the undefeated Pittsfield Lions, and by the fourth quarter, they'd amassed a twenty-five-point lead over their rivals. With victory in the bag, the coach subbed in Pat Kenward, a severely autistic student who had spent the past four seasons volunteering as a water boy. That's when Vince had stepped in.

"You're telling me you didn't like watching it?" Vince asked Eliza.

"I just think it was a little over the top," she said.

As soon as Pat received the ball, he let loose from the three-point line. The ball ricocheted wildly off the backboard—and somehow bounced into the net. The crowd erupted into applause, nearly hysterical with joy.

"You could've stopped at one shot," Eliza told Vince. "It would've been just as inspiring."

The Archangel grinned. "I don't know about that."

The coach was about to remove Pat from the game, satisfied that he'd done his duty. But before he could call a time-out, an errant ball slid into the autistic boy's hand. Confused, he fired the ball wildly toward the basket from half-court. It fell through the hoop in a perfect swish. The crowd reacted with glee—and then shock—

as Pat continued to drain threes. By the end of the game, he'd scored nearly forty points.

"Disney optioned it for a movie," Vince said proudly.

He stood up and headed for the vending machines. He was almost out the door when he tilted his head back toward Eliza.

"*Disney,*" he repeated.

"That guy's a total hack," she whispered to Craig when the Archangel was safely out of earshot.

"Please don't antagonize him," Craig begged. "I had to flatter him for thirty straight minutes before he'd agree to help us."

"I just don't understand why we even *need* him."

"Look," Craig said, "I know Vince can be a little sloppy. But what do you expect? He's an executive, an ideas guy. It's his job to shake things up."

"He's just so *cocky.*"

"I know," Craig said. "But maybe that's the kind of confidence we need right now?"

He opened his laptop and located Raoul, standing outside a Jack in the Box, dressed in women's underwear and wrapped in a large gray tarp.

"The End Is Near," his sign read. "The World Will End in Fourteen Days."

Craig looked into Eliza's eyes. "We're running out of time."

* * *

Vince flipped through Craig's research.

"This Cliff guy seems pretty cool," he said. "Cool beard, sick pickup lines. No wonder he's rolling in pussy."

Eliza shot Craig a look.

"We need to get him out of the picture," Craig explained to Vince. "Otherwise Sam won't have a shot."

The Archangel nodded. "We could just kill him," he suggested casually.

Craig coughed. "That might be a little much. I was thinking, maybe we could just get him to leave New York City?"

Vince shrugged. "Even easier."

He slowly reclined in his chair and closed his eyes.

"Eliza, take this down."

"I'm not your secretary."

"I'll take it down," Craig murmured.

He took out a pad and pencil and watched as Vince Blake went to work.

EARTH—ELEVEN DAYS UNTIL DOOMSDAY

Cliff Davenport smiled proudly at his purchase. He'd never seen a prewar Underwood typewriter in such perfect condition. It was so sleek, so elegant, so *authentic.* It was just what he needed to finally start writing his novel.

He'd tried to compose the work on a computer, but there was something so soulless about modern technology. It sucked all the romance out of the process. Literature wasn't something you cranked out on a mass-produced laptop, like some corporate spreadsheet. He'd given up halfway through the first sentence.

Now, after six months of searching, he'd finally found a suitable writing instrument. He could begin his novel at once. All he needed was some ink, some ribbons, a ream of soft French paper, a pleasant office, a comfy leather chair, a simple oak desk, a vase or two of fresh-cut flowers, and a bottle of overproof absinthe to stimulate his imagination. He hadn't yet arrived at a subject for his novel, but he was sure one would come to him in time.

"It's four thousand bucks," said the gruff-voiced clerk behind the counter.

Cliff smiled sympathetically at the merchant. The poor man obviously knew nothing of art. His life was a coarse one, a moment-to-moment, animalistic struggle for survival. He spent his days among beautiful typewriters, but to him they were merely "goods"—inert pieces of metal to be bought and sold like any other commodity. The irony nearly brought tears to Cliff's eyes.

"Your Visa's not going through," the man told him.

Cliff smiled. "There must be some mistake."

"I tried it three times."

"Huh," Cliff said. "Well... here's my AmEx."

He watched with some anxiety as the shopkeeper swiped his card—then reswiped it.

"No dice," he said. "Sorry, kid." He picked up the typewriter with a grunt and lugged it back to the shopwindow.

"You must've done it wrong," Cliff said. "Pressed the wrong button or something."

The shopkeeper folded his arms impatiently. "Do you want me to swipe it again?"

"No," Cliff said, collecting himself. "I'll be back in just a minute."

He staggered outside and shakily lit a hand-rolled cigarette. After a few long drags, he worked up the courage to call his father.

"Clifford, where the hell have you been?" the old man shouted. "I must've called a dozen times."

"I've been busy," Cliff said. "Listen—there's a problem with my credit cards. They don't seem to be working."

"I know. I canceled them."

"What?"

"Jesus, Clifford! Have you listened to any of my voice mails?"

Cliff admitted that he hadn't.

"The company's in shambles," his father informed him. "My net worth has dropped eighty percent in three days. This fiasco has ruined us!"

"What fiasco?"

His father cursed under his breath. "Haven't you been watching the news?"

"I don't own a television," Cliff said proudly.

"Well, I'll fill you in when you get home. Just take some cash out of the machine and buy a ticket back to Michigan. And fly *coach*, for God's sake! This bohemian lifestyle of yours isn't going to cut it anymore."

Cliff gritted his teeth. "I see," he said. "Because I've chosen an artistic path, I'm being cut off. Cast out."

"What? No—I just can't pay your rent anymore."

"I don't need you to support me," Cliff declared. "All great artists go through periods of poverty. All I need to survive are a few blank sheets of paper, a brush, and a little loft to store my canvases."

"Your little loft is costing me twenty-nine hundred bucks a month. I'm sorry, kiddo. You've got to come home."

"But Dad, I want to stay!"

Cliff bit his lip, embarrassed by his childish outburst. "I'm sorry for ranting," he said, in as deep a voice as he could muster. "It's just, when I think about my art, I get so fired up. It's like a flame inside my heart that won't stop burning."

"What the hell does that mean?"

Cliff sighed. "I don't know," he admitted.

* * *

"I told you it'd be easy," Vince said, kicking his feet up onto Eliza's desk.

Craig scrolled through the figures in shock; in just three days, Vince had practically bankrupted Cliff's family. The Davenports were so financially destitute that Cliff would have to live at home indefinitely. There was even a chance he would have to find some kind of job.

"That was fast," Eliza conceded. "But I still think the way you handled it was pretty crass."

"It's not crass if it works."

They both glanced at Craig, clearly waiting for him to take a side.

He flashed them an awkward smile. "I think it's time for some more coffee."

He hurried off to the break room, threw on a pot, and waited for it to percolate. He agreed with Eliza; Vince's miracle was one of the most tasteless things he'd ever witnessed.

That said, he couldn't fault the Archangel's reasoning. The Davenport fortune was almost completely wrapped up in Americo Pastries Company stock. If you wanted to bankrupt them, you had to devalue their company's shares. And the only way to do that was to tarnish the company's image.

For over thirty years, Regis Philbin had served as the official spokesperson for the Americo Pastries Company. He was the public face of the brand, even more than Cliff's father. Vince had zeroed in on him immediately.

"We're gonna use Regis good," he pronounced ominously. "We're gonna use him real good."

Regis Philbin had recently agreed to plug APC on his live morning show. The company was launching a new product—Banana Bread Bonanza—and was counting on him to unveil it to the world. He began the promotional segment by extolling the new product's taste ("It ain't too sweet—or too sour!"). Then, to prove that his praise was genuine, the elderly talk show host happily swallowed a sample. Within three seconds he began to vomit. The look of shock on Regis's face, coupled with the intensity of the vomiting, turned the incident into a YouTube sensation. After 23 million views, Philbin had no choice but to release a statement.

> For the past three decades, it has been my great privilege to serve as the North American spokesman for Americo Pastries. I would just like to make clear that the sickness I experienced on my show this morning had nothing to do with the quality of that company's product. Americo has always produced top-notch pastries that are delicious, nutritious, and fun for the whole family. Their taste and value can't be beat. Tomorrow morning on my show I will repeat the segment so that everyone can see there is nothing to fear.

The following morning 2.8 million viewers were watching as Regis took his seat, surrounded by an array of Americo muffins and Danishes. After reading and responding to a few get-well cards from celebrities, he tried one of the Danishes and immediately started vomiting again. This time it was the velocity more than the volume that astonished viewers; the vomit arced out of his mouth in a perfect parabola—landing on the other side of the stage. It was almost as if it had hit some kind of invisible wind current.

Regis's next statement was shorter:

> In my rush to clear the good name of Americo Pastries, I did not take into account the severity of my illness. I have decided to take a day off from work, during which the network will be showing "The Best of Regis," featuring all the stars and segments you've come to love. When I return, I will complete the Americo Pastries segment so that we can all move on from these unfortunate events.

Over 9 million Americans woke up early to watch Regis's return, making it the highest-rated morning television broadcast since the coverage of Princess Diana's funeral. Regis, clearly anxious to get the segment over with as quickly as possible, chose to forgo his customary introduction. Instead, he walked straight out onto the set and took a seat in front of the pastries.

"Third time's a charm!" he said, prompting polite laughter from the studio audience.

The studio fell into a hushed silence as Regis inched his hand toward the plate. He started to reach for a Danish, then hesitated, clearly traumatized by his recent experiences. After a lengthy pause, he selected a simple corn muffin from the tray. He was smiling when he bit into it, but as many YouTube commentators would later point out, there was an unmistakable look of terror in his eyes. The first bite went down cleanly, and for a moment Regis seemed to relax. No sooner had he leaned back in his chair, however, than a torrent of vomit spewed volcanically out of his screaming mouth.

The next official statement came from Philbin's lawyer.

> Regis Philbin has decided not to renew his contract as North American spokesman of the Americo Pastries Company and will be moving on.

FDA scientists could find nothing wrong with the pastries. Regis had simply gotten spontaneously sick on three separate occasions, a random victim of various airborne pathogens. But it was too outlandish a coincidence; everyone blamed Americo. The company had no choice but to issue a mass recall of its pastries to allay consumers' fears. The stock fell nearly 85 percent.

* * *

Craig hid in the break room for as long as he could, but when he returned to his cubicle, the air was still thick with conflict.

"He's an old man," Eliza was saying. "Can you imagine how frightening all this must have been for him? One moment he's fine—the next moment he's vomiting?"

Vince grinned slyly. "Come on," he said. "You've got to admit it was entertaining."

"It was revolting!"

"Guys, please," Craig interrupted. "What's done is done, and we don't have time to argue."

He pulled up Raoul on his computer, and the prophet's cardboard sign made him gasp.

"'The World Will End in Eight Days,'" Eliza read. "I can't believe this—we're down to single digits!"

"Huh," Vince said. "Then I guess I better stop holding back."

Craig put down his coffee mug and rose to his feet for the first time in twelve hours. He'd been working for so long that his dress shirt had adhered to his chair. It made a disgusting sound when he stood up, like a Band-Aid being ripped off a wound.

"Did you crack it?" Eliza asked hopefully.

"Not quite."

She nodded. Two Chance Encounters in two weeks was a lot to expect from any Angel, even one as brilliant as Craig.

"What's tripping you up?" Vince asked.

"I don't know. There are just too many variables."

He grabbed a pad of paper from his desk and drew a rough map of the Lower East Side.

"Sam's apartment is here," he explained, drawing a stick figure at the corner of Ludlow and Delancey.

"And Laura lives *here.*" He drew a long-haired stick figure on the corner of Forsyth and Stanton. "That means, technically, she's on his way to work. Should be easy, right? But here's the thing—they *never* cross paths."

"Why not?" Vince asked.

"Two reasons. First, Laura almost never leaves her apartment. Sam could sit on her front stoop for hours and still not run into her. Second of all, Sam never walks to work. He always takes the subway."

"But it's only eight blocks away."

"I know," Eliza said. "He's incredibly lazy."

"What if the weather's nice?" Vince asked.

Craig sighed. "It doesn't matter if it's seventy-two degrees and sunny. He won't do it."

"Wow." Vince wrinkled his nose. "I'm surprised he isn't fatter."

"We gave him salmonella," Eliza explained.

Vince raised his eyebrows, impressed, and Eliza smiled proudly in spite of herself.

"Anyway," Craig said, "I've figured out a way to get Laura outside."

He pulled up her apartment on his computer and zoomed in on her crumpled jeans.

"She wears these same filthy jeans every day. And the pockets are falling apart." He clicked his mouse a few times, zeroing in on her left buttock.

"See?" he said, pointing at the tattered fabric. "It's full of holes. All I have to do is force some contact—make her slip on the sidewalk or something—and her keys will fall right through."

"That's perfect!" Eliza said. "She'll have to call her super and wait for him outside the front door."

"Exactly. She'll be set in a specific location."

"What about Sam?" Vince interrupted. "How do you get him to walk by?"

"I don't know," Craig admitted. "Like I said, he always takes the F train to work—one stop, from Essex to Second Avenue. It's not like we can tell him to stop doing that."

Vince grinned. "What if we stopped the train?"

Eliza squinted at him suspiciously. "How?"

The Archangel shrugged. "I don't know. A crash, maybe? Or an earthquake?"

Eliza rolled her eyes. She was about to change the subject when Craig interrupted her.

"We could easily crash the F," he said. "Just a couple of brake jams, and we could knock it right out of commission."

"Easy peasy," Vince agreed.

Eliza stared at her colleagues in shock. "You're actually considering crashing the F train?"

Craig nodded glumly. "We might have to. You know what a fat ass Sam is. As long as that train is running, he's going to ride it."

"I know," Eliza said. "But if there's a crash, won't that cause other problems? We're talking about fire trucks and ambulances—hundreds of vehicles descending on the Lower East Side. What if some cop barricades Sam's path?"

Craig sighed. "You're right. It's too risky."

The three of them sat for a minute in silence.

"You know," Craig said cautiously, "there is another way to stop the train. But it would take some real doing."

He pulled up a recent *New York Post* article. The MTA was right in the middle of contract negotiations with the union, and the annual budget was due in thirty-six hours. Both sides were "optimistic" about reaching an agreement. But if talks broke down somehow, and the deadline passed, every train in New York would be grounded.

"A transit strike could work," Eliza said. "But how can we cause the sides to disagree?"

"Yeah," Craig said. "It's not like we can control their thoughts."

"That's true," Vince said. "But maybe we can control their moods."

He slid his swivel chair over to Craig's computer and grabbed the mouse.

"Why don't you two take a coffee break?" he said. "I've got this one under control."

Vince scanned the globe. People everywhere were flipping through newspapers, asking tough questions, debating the issues of the day. He laughed to himself. The humans believed that they were rational creatures, governed by their values and belief systems. In fact, almost all of their choices were based on what they had eaten for breakfast, whether or not they had slept well, and how long it had been since their last satisfactory orgasm.

In Vince's opinion, these three factors—breakfast, sleep, orgasm—accounted for most events in human history. Benedict Arnold was a naturally sour person. But he never would have betrayed his country had it not been for the mosquitoes in his bedroom, depriving him of sleep for weeks and stripping his mind of reason. The Magna Carta might have been an ingenious document. But King John never would have signed it had it not been for his teenage mistress and the generous mood she engendered in her aging ruler.

An undercooked sausage, a snoring spouse—these were the events that shaped the world. Governors were three times more likely to sign a death warrant if they hadn't had their coffee yet. And surgeons performed best when they were in love. There were other factors at play in human decision-making—allergies, bowel regularity, and headaches, for instance. But almost all were biological and remarkably easy to manipulate. Any Angel worth his wings could do it.

He stared at the screen. A dozen lawyers from the MTA and the Transport Workers Union had gathered in a City Hall conference room. Neither side wanted a strike, but Vince had done his best to make everybody as ornery as possible. His first move was to break an overhead steam pipe. The room's temperature was eighty-six degrees and climbing fast. None of the lawyers wanted to remove their jackets—taking off one's clothes could be interpreted as a sign of weakness. But the heat eventually became unbearable. At the ten-hour mark, the lawyers came to a mutual agreement to remove their coats. Four hours later, they agreed to strip to their undershirts. At the twenty-hour mark, one of the junior counsels became so overheated that he pulled his superior aside and asked if he could remove his undershirt and go naked from the waist up. When his request was denied, he walked into the bathroom and passed out.

Vince had also jammed a smoke detector, causing it to beep abrasively every three and a half minutes. The interval was timed to cause the lawyers maximum annoyance: each beep arrived just seconds after they'd forgotten about the last one.

Vince had known in advance which lawyers would attend the meeting and had spent the previous couple of days torturing them. By the time they arrived in the sweltering bunker, their nerves were frayed and their tempers short. Of the six union lawyers, five had the flu, three had ingrown toenails, and two had undiagnosed mono. He'd given the other side a mixture of sunburn, cold sores, and ear infections. The mediator, usually a cheerful presence, remained completely silent for the entire meeting. Vince had given him a case of gonorrhea so horrific that whenever he went to the bathroom, he had to bite his tie to keep from screaming.

By the thirty-six-hour mark, no progress had been made. Every single debate seemed to degenerate into childish bickering.

With a strike imminent, the chief union lawyer struggled to his feet.

"So?" he challenged, his voice scratchy from a bacterial infection. "What's it going to be? Are you going to agree to our demands or what?"

The lead MTA lawyer looked up wearily. His eyes were bleary from allergies. He was about to respond when a cloud of pollen wafted toward his nose. He sneezed a few times, recovered, and then began to sneeze again, for over a minute straight. When the attack was finally over, he stood up, held his fists above his head, and let loose a wild, uninhibited scream. Then he sat back down and buried his face in his hands.

The strike mediator shifted uncomfortably in his seat. "Okay," he said. "I guess for now we can agree to disagree."

EARTH—TWO DAYS UNTIL DOOMSDAY

Laura lay on the icy pavement, dazed and disoriented. It took her a second or two to make sense of her situation: she'd slipped on a frozen puddle and was lying on the sidewalk.

Laura was a clumsy person and fell down pretty often. Still, it always took her by surprise. There was something so shocking about falling. One moment you were completely in control of your limbs. A split second later you were flailing through the air, as spastic as a swatted mosquito.

She spotted a yellow bus and realized with horror that she'd fallen down in front of a school. She could hear the children laughing at her, and when she looked up, she realized that they were mimicking her fall—arms swinging wildly, faces contorted, butts extended. A middle-aged teacher yelled at them to stop, but their impressions were pretty good, and before long he was laughing too.

Laura struggled to her feet with as much dignity as she could muster and fled the scene. She was moving so quickly that it took her five blocks to discover her pocket had ripped open and the keys to her apartment were missing.

She desperately retraced her steps, scanning the ground for shiny objects. But a freak October blizzard had emerged out of nowhere, blanketing the city with snow. The keys were lost for good. There was nothing to do but call the super and wait for him to let her in.

She sat on her stoop, idly scanning old text messages to pass the time. Cliff had sent her a cryptic one a few days ago: "NYC is a soulless town, full of corporate zombies. i must return 2 my birthplace 2 purify my soul." She couldn't make much sense of it, but she figured she wouldn't be seeing him for a while.

She was debating whether to text him back when she heard a familiar sneeze. She looked up and laughed with surprise.

"Sam? Is that you?"

"Laura! Oh my God, what a coincidence!"

The blizzard had been raging for hours, but as Sam shuffled across the icy street, the weather seemed to improve. By the time he got to her stoop, the snow had completely stopped and the sun had emerged for the first time all day.

"What a crazy coincidence!" he repeated. "I never would've walked by here if it hadn't been for the strike!"

"I know! This is so . . . random!"

They stood for a moment in silence.

"Well!" he said. "I guess I should get going."

"Oh," she said, her voice tinged with obvious disappointment. "Well, it was nice running into you."

"Same! I guess...I'll see you around?"

"Yeah! I'm sure I'll see ya."

They embraced awkwardly, their arms almost fully extended.

"Bye!" Sam said.

He was about to walk away when a jagged chunk of ice fell onto his face.

"Fuck!"

He collapsed on the ground, screaming with fear and pain. "Oh fuck!"

Laura knelt down beside him. "Jesus, Sam—are you okay?"

"No!"

"What in God's name *was* that?"

"It felt like a fucking knife!"

She spotted an icicle near his face.

"It must've been this thing," she said, lifting up the gleaming spike.

Sam's eyelids fluttered slightly; he was about to faint.

"Let me see your cheek," Laura said, prying Sam's fingers off his face. "Oh, geez...you're bleeding."

"I am?" Sam cried, his voice shrill with panic. "Oh my God!"

"It's okay," she said. "It's not so bad."

She rubbed her finger across his wound. The cut was small, but the flesh around it had already started to darken.

"You'll probably have a black eye," she told him. "But it'll be fine in a day or two."

Sam lowered his eyes. It looked like he was blushing, though it was hard to tell because his face was so discolored.

"Sorry for losing it," he murmured.

"That's okay—I would've lost it too! That thing was like the size of a sword."

They sat for a moment in silence. The snow-speckled sidewalk shimmered in the sunlight, and a fuzzy rainbow arced overhead. Sam made eye contact with Laura, and she anxiously batted her eyes.

"Hey," he ventured, "maybe we could grab coffee sometime? You know... someplace *indoors.*"

Laura laughed. "Yeah," she said. "That'd be fun."

Across the street, a fire hydrant suddenly erupted. Sam laughed. He knew it was crazy, but it seemed like some kind of a sign.

"Another round!" Vince shouted.

Craig nodded and poured out three glasses of bourbon.

"That siren at the end was a nice touch," Vince said.

Craig grinned. "I couldn't resist."

"And Eliza, that icicle was badass."

"Thanks," she said. "I didn't want to hurt him, but I had no choice. He was about to bail."

Vince nodded. "He's such a fucking pussy."

"Hey, come on," Craig said. "He asked her out, right? That took some guts."

"He didn't 'ask her out,'" Eliza said. "He asked her if she wanted to 'grab coffee sometime.'"

"That's asking her out," Craig said.

"No, it's not! Asking someone out is 'Do you want to go on a date with me?' It's not 'Do you want to grab coffee?' I mean, *you* ask me that five times a day."

Craig's face reddened. After a moment, so did Eliza's.

"Well," Vince said, grinning slyly. "At least we're making progress, right?"

He threw his arms around their shoulders and raised his glass. "To courtship!"

"To courtship," they mumbled.

They finished their drinks, and Vince immediately refilled them. Their hands were still shaking from the stress of the last fifteen minutes. They'd worked non-stop for days—spreading flu, manipulating storm clouds, melting icicles—and the humans had almost blown it once again.

"Demolition is scheduled for tomorrow," Craig said. "Midnight, Eastern Standard Time. So Sam and Laura's date...or, you know, whatever it is. It's got to go well."

Vince and Eliza nodded solemnly.

"Get some sleep," Craig told them. "Tomorrow is a big day."

Vince put on his jacket, and Craig followed him over to the elevators.

"You coming?" he asked Eliza.

She shook her head. "I'm going to stick around for a couple of minutes. There's something I need to take care of."

EARTH—TWENTY-THREE HOURS UNTIL DOOMSDAY

Laura ran frantically through the halls of her high school. She was late for something—her sister's wedding, possibly. And someone had replaced the hallways with city sidewalks, which was extremely inconvenient. She was trying to climb a ladder made of icicles when she felt someone gripping her ankle. She looked down and saw a tired, thin woman with brown bangs. Her clothes were stained with coffee, and her mascara was smudged and faded. But there was something arresting about her. Her blue eyes seemed unnaturally bright, and her pale skin looked almost like it was glowing.

"Do I know you?" Laura asked.

The woman awkwardly thrust out her hand.

"I'm Eliza," she said. "I'm sorry—I've never done this before." She cleared her throat. "I'm an Angel."

"Oh, I get it." Laura said. "So this is a..."

Eliza nodded. "Yeah. Listen...is there somewhere we can talk?"

Laura led her down Third Avenue to her high school cafeteria. They sat across from each other, and Eliza summed up the situation as fast as she could. By the time she was finished, she was almost out of breath.

"Why us?" Laura asked.

"I told you," Eliza said. "Because you both prayed to be together."

She gripped the human's elbow.

"Just make a move," she begged. "You've got to. Everything is riding on it. Sam likes you, but he's way too shy to do anything about it, and you're running out of time."

Laura smirked. "Why don't *you* make a move?"

"What are you talking about?"

"That Craig guy. You're obviously into him. You called him a genius. Twice."

"Craig's just a colleague," she said defensively. "And besides—this isn't about me."

"Why don't you just ask him out?" Laura pressed. "Say, 'Let's take a break from this Angel stuff and go out on a date.' It's 2012. You don't need to wait for him to do it."

Eliza chewed on her thumbnail.

"Okay," she said. "How about this? If you and Sam make it work tomorrow—and the world doesn't end—I'll go on a date with Craig."

Laura playfully shook Eliza's hand, but when she caught sight of the Angel's bloodshot eyes, her face turned pale.

"Oh my God," she whispered. "This is real."

Eliza gripped her fingers tightly. "This is real," she said.

A car commercial blared through the school's PA system.

"1-877-KARS4KIDS, K-A-R-S KARS4KIDS..."

Laura rolled over, opened her eyes, and smacked the snooze alarm.

Her sheets were damp with sweat.

She wondered what it was she'd been dreaming about.

Eliza got to work at 6 a.m., but Craig was already there.

"Get any sleep?" she asked.

Craig shook his head. "Not really."

He was watching something on his computer, a queasy expression on his face.

"What're you doing?" she asked.

"Research."

She sat down beside him. On the screen, Sam was dancing alone in his apartment to a song by ABBA. He was completely naked.

She grimaced. "I don't see how watching this will help us."

"I know it's pretty rough," Craig agreed. "But we

need to learn as much about these humans as possible. Any insight into their character might help."

He gestured at Sam's gyrating body. "For instance. Now we know that Sam enjoys dancing. But we *also* know that he's bad at it. That means we need to prevent him from dancing in front of Laura—if possible."

"He's also bad at sex," Vince interrupted.

Craig and Eliza looked up at him.

"How do you know that?" Craig asked.

"I went through the Server last night," Vince said, "and I watched every sexual encounter he's ever had."

"Wow," Eliza said. "How long did that take you?"

Vince chuckled. "Not long."

Eliza scrunched her face up with disgust. "What was it like?"

"It was horrible," Vince said. "Honestly, some of the most upsetting images I've ever seen. And I've watched most of World War Two."

"What was so bad about it?"

"I'll spare you the specifics. Suffice it to say he lacks confidence."

He grabbed Craig's keyboard and logged on to the Server.

"The female's better in bed," he said. "But she's just as bad on dates."

He opened a clip from earlier in the year. Laura was standing in front of a jukebox next to a bearded man in a sweater.

"Who's she with?"

"Some guy her sister set her up with," Vince explained. "He just put a dollar into the machine and asked her to pick a song."

They watched as Laura scrolled through the options, a panicked expression on her face.

"What's taking her so long?"

"She's terrified," Vince said. "Watch this."

He turned up the volume, and the Angels leaned in toward the screen.

"Well, what do you want to listen to?" Laura asked.

"I don't know," he said. *"Anything."*

"Do you like Ace of Base?"

"Why, do you like them?"

"I don't know! Do you... not *like them?"*

Vince turned off the clip. "It goes on like that for ten minutes. Eventually, the guy's dollar expires."

Craig checked his watch. "It's six-fifteen," he said. "That means we have less than eighteen hours."

Vince smirked. "If I was down there, I wouldn't need eighteen *minutes.*"

He popped his collar and slicked back his hair.

"I'd get there ten minutes late, just to keep her on edge. Then, just when she was starting to panic, I'd stroll in. I wouldn't apologize. I'd just head straight to the bar and order two martinis."

He pushed Craig's swivel chair out of the way and crouched down beside Eliza. "Then I'd propose a toast."

He raised his coffee mug; Eliza laughed and jokingly raised her water bottle.

Vince leaned toward her. "I'd say, 'Now, usually I toast to world peace. But I'm distracted by how incredible you look. So tonight we'll toast to your beauty. And the world can go to hell.' "

Craig scoffed. "That would never work."

He turned to Eliza for confirmation, but she remained strangely silent. Her eyes were locked on Vince's and her lips were slightly parted.

"Then I'd take her hand," Vince continued in a low voice. "And lean across the table."

Craig winced as Vince took Eliza's hand and pressed his mouth against Eliza's ear. He whispered something, and her cheeks subtly reddened.

"Okay," Craig said. "You're very smooth and cool. Congratulations. Can we maybe get back to saving the world now?"

"Of course," Vince said. He took the keyboard and looked up the two humans. It wasn't even seven yet, but both of them were already parked in front of their computers.

"How are we going to get these people to *kiss?*" Eliza said. "They're the most unappealing humans I've ever seen."

"I've been thinking about that," Craig said. "And there is one thing that might help."

"What?"

"Alcohol."

Vince shook his head. "That's not going to help us."

"Why not?" Craig said. "Alcohol has been scientifically proven to lower inhibitions and increase libido. Almost every couple is somewhat intoxicated during their first kiss."

"That might be true," Vince said. "But we can't just force-feed ethanol down these people's throats."

"We can try," Craig said, a slight edge in his voice.

"How? They're meeting at a Dunkin Donuts."

Craig looked at his watch. "We'll have to burn it down," he said.

Vince laughed incredulously. "What?"

"We'll burn the Dunkin Donuts down. And if the humans try to relocate to some other bullshit coffee place, we'll burn *that* place down. And we'll keep on burning places down until they get their heads in the game and go to a bar like a couple of fucking adults!"

He stood up suddenly, his jaw muscles clenched with determination.

"I'm sick of pussyfooting around here! It's time to make this *happen.* Are you guys with me on this or not?"

Vince gave a startled nod and turned toward Eliza. She was smiling at Craig, her eyes bright with admiration.

"I'm with you," she said.

Craig sat down and zoomed in tight on the Lower East Side.

"We can do this," he said. "Just follow my lead."

EARTH—SEVEN HOURS UNTIL DOOMSDAY

Sam stood in front of the bathroom mirror, trying his best not to hyperventilate. He knew it wasn't even a real date, just a friendly trip to Dunkin Donuts. Still, the stakes felt strangely high.

He posed awkwardly in front of his mirror. He was wearing his favorite outfit: a cable-knit sweater and khakis.

"Don't worry," he said out loud to his panicky reflection. "You look great."

"He looks *awful,*" Vince said.

"I've never seen less flattering clothes," Eliza said. "Look at how those khakis bunch around his ass."

"It's okay," Craig said. "I'm on it."

EARTH—SIX HOURS AND FORTY-FIVE MINUTES UNTIL DOOMSDAY

"Oh, fuck!" Sam shouted.

He stared with horror at his sauce-speckled clothes. He'd been reheating some leftover chicken vindaloo when a sauce bubble suddenly exploded, splattering his pants and sweater.

He was dolefully changing into jeans when he heard his ringtone. He grabbed his dirty khakis and rummaged through the pockets for his iPhone. His heart raced with panic: was Laura canceling on him? He took a deep breath, bracing himself for disappointment.

> To Sam
> From Laura
> Sam, hi! This is crazy, but the Dunkin Donuts burned to the ground! Do you want to meet at Last Call for happy hour?

Sam sat on the foot of his bed, sighing heavily with relief.

> To Laura
> From Sam
> On my way!

Sam's stomach growled audibly. He'd been too nervous to eat breakfast or lunch and now there wasn't time to eat dinner. He checked his hair in the mirror, ran out the door, and trotted down the street to Last Call.

He ran inside the bar and scanned the room for Laura, but she hadn't arrived yet. There was nothing to do but wait. He sat down at a table near the back, then quickly moved to another, concerned that the first one was located too close to the bathroom. A few minutes later, he noticed that his new table was slightly sticky. He moved again.

* * *

"Oh, man," Vince said. "He's freaking out."

"Why'd he get there so early?" Eliza said.

She typed Laura's name into Omnex. The female was still taking a shower.

"Look at how much Sam's sweating," Craig said. "At this rate, he'll have a full-fledged panic attack before she even shows."

"Hey, look," Vince said. "He's finally going to the bar."

He watched hopefully as the human flipped through the cocktail menu.

"He'd better order something stiff."

EARTH—FIVE AND A HALF HOURS UNTIL DOOMSDAY

"I'll try the Lemondrop," Sam said.

The bearded bartender glared at him with undisguised contempt.

"The *Lemondrop*?"

Sam smiled apologetically. "I'm not much of a drinker."

The bartender reached beneath the counter and pulled out a dusty leather-bound book. After a few minutes of searching, he located the recipe.

"Sorry if it's a hard one!" Sam said.

The bartender ignored him and poured some lemon juice into a blender. Then he added simple syrup, and three maraschino cherries. He was carefully adding the gin when the nozzle fell off of his Seagram's bottle.

"Shit," he said. "Good gin wasted."

He squinted at Sam. "Hope you don't mind a double."

"Of course not!" Sam replied, trying his best not to be rude. "Thank you!"

"Nice one," Vince said. "How much of that sweet stuff do you think made it in there?"

Craig zoomed in on Sam's cocktail and analyzed its chemical makeup.

"Three ounces of gin," he declared.

Vince and Eliza applauded.

"On an empty stomach, too," Craig noted.

The cubicle suddenly fell silent—Laura had finally arrived. The Angels watched with rapt attention as the humans hugged and laughed, prattling on about their boring days.

"I can't believe she's still wearing those awful jeans," Eliza whispered. "Doesn't she have any self-respect at all?"

"Her ass looks like a spider's web," Vince said.

"Quiet," Craig said. "I don't want to miss anything."

He turned up the volume as loud as it would go.

EARTH—TWO AND A HALF HOURS UNTIL DOOMSDAY

"Wait," Sam said. "So people think you're a radio station?"

Laura nodded. "101.1 FM."

"And you give away fake prizes?"

"I know I should stop. It's just...when they get their prizes, they're always so *excited.* They laugh and scream." She lowered her eyes and shrugged. "I guess sometimes it's nice to feel like you have the power to make someone happy." She peered up at Sam self-consciously. "Is that crazy?"

"No," Sam said, thinking of the pleasure he felt when he handed his drunken boss lottery tickets. "I think I know what you mean."

She smiled at him and he felt a brief sense of calm. But within a few seconds, his anxiety returned in full force, like a tidal wave returning to the shore. She'd finished her beer, he noticed, but hadn't yet ordered a second one. Did that mean she was bored with him and gearing up to leave? She probably had a party to go to or something.

"Wow, look at the time!" he said, awkwardly giving her an out. "I can't believe how long we've been sitting here."

Laura's eyes widened with panic. "Do you have to be somewhere?"

"No!" he said, frantically. "No—I don't have any plans."

He chewed his lower lip, struggling to regain his composure. "What about you?"

"No," she said, blushing. "This is all I've got."

"Two more hours!" Brian chanted.

He was wearing a colorful party hat and holding a bag of kazoos. He pulled out a handful and tossed them into Craig's cubicle.

"You guys want to do body shots with me?" he asked.

Craig shook his head. "We're busy."

"Then I guess I'll see you at the party."

Eliza glared at him. "What party?"

"The End of the World party! We're going to watch demolition in the break room."

He blew his kazoo. "Do you think he'll use fire or ice? Someone in Accounts started a pool."

"I don't know," Vince muttered.

"Yeah, I don't really care myself. It's going to be a pretty sick explosion either way."

The Angels glared at Brian as he lurched toward the break room. When he opened the door, a blast of music blared across the office. It sounded like Lynyrd Skynyrd.

"Is *God* at that party?" Eliza asked.

"Probably," Vince said.

"Let's just focus," Craig urged them. "We're running out of time."

He swiveled toward the screen and gasped in panic.

"Oh no," he said. "Oh, crap."

"What?" Eliza demanded. "What's wrong?"

Craig shook his head in misery. "I think Sam's about to dance."

EARTH—NINETY MINUTES UNTIL DOOMSDAY

Sam rocked unsteadily to his feet, nearly spilling his fourth Lemondrop of the evening.

"I can't believe you picked Ace of Base!" he shouted. "They're, like, my all-time favorite group!"

Laura beamed. "Really? You like them?"

"I *love* them!"

He wobbled toward the jukebox and began to move to the music, thrusting out his groin in time with the beat. He gyrated for a minute, clapping his hands at random intervals. When the song reached the chorus, he spun around in a tight circle, pointing and winking at imaginary people.

"I saw the sign," he sang atonally. *"It opened up my eyes, I saw the sign!"*

"I'm going to start a fire," Craig said.

"You can't!" Eliza protested. "The kitchen's full of workers—they'll be engulfed in flames!"

"I don't care who dies," Craig said. "This needs to stop right now."

Eliza faced the screen. Sam was punching the air with his fists now, shaking his hips in time with the music. Every few beats, he stretched out his palm and playfully slapped his buttocks.

"You're right," she muttered.

Craig grabbed the keyboard and typed in a fire code, pressurizing the oven past capacity. It was about to burst into flames when Vince grabbed his elbow.

"Wait!" He pointed at the screen. "Look."

The Angels realized with shock that Laura had joined Sam on the dance floor. Her palms were stretched to the ceiling in a "raise the roof" pose, and her head was shaking spastically to the beat.

"Holy shit," Eliza said. "She's just as bad as he is."

They leaned back in their chairs and watched with amazement as the humans circled one another, mirroring each other's terrible movements. Their dancing was flawed in all the same ways. And even though neither could follow the song's rhythm, their limbs twitched in time with each other's.

When the final chorus began, Laura mimed a microphone with her fist and held it up to Sam's face. He grabbed her wrist and sang terribly into her fingers. The song ended and they burst into laughter, oblivious to the stares of the regulars and the bartender's sarcastic applause.

"Want to get out of here?" Laura asked breathlessly.

Sam's smile faded and the blood drained from his face. "Okay," he said.

She headed for the door, and he followed her out into the night.

Craig turned to his colleagues, his eyelids twitching with anxiety.

"What do we do now?" Eliza asked.

"We watch," he said.

A large crashing noise rang out from the break room, followed by a rowdy cheer. "Sweet Home Alabama" was playing on a continuous loop, and whenever the opening guitar riff sounded, the entire party burst into uproarious applause.

"Everybody get naked!" Brian was chanting, his voice somewhat hoarse from screaming. *"Naked!"*

Craig opened a new window and typed in a search for God's prophet, Raoul. He found him at a Taco Bell in Flushing. He was sitting alone at a booth, staring at an enormous pile of food. He'd bought over a dozen tacos, along with a family-size tub of nachos, and some kind of chocolate gordita. The Angels watched as the prophet took his Timex off his wrist. He placed the watch beside his soda, reached for a plastic fork, and calmly began to eat.

"Oh my God," Eliza whispered. "Is he . . . ?"

Craig nodded. "He's having his last meal."

Craig zoomed out from the Taco Bell, and then from

Flushing, and then New York until the continent began to take shape: the jagged Eastern Seaboard, the murky ocean, the hazy wisp of atmosphere overhead. Soon they could see the entire planet, a bluish ball, splotched with green, studded with shimmering cities.

Craig clicked his mouse, zooming in tight on the Lower East Side. The humans had just left Last Call. It was 11:06 p.m.

"Come on," he whispered at the screen. "Come on, you guys. Don't blow it."

EARTH—FIFTY-FOUR MINUTES UNTIL DOOMSDAY

Sam and Laura stood outside Last Call, awkwardly avoiding eye contact.

"I usually go this way," Sam said. "What about you?"

"Same," she lied.

"Great!" Sam said, a little too loudly. "That's great!"

They moved slowly down the avenue, staying about two arms' lengths apart. Sam realized with terror that they were already at Delancey Street. If he was going to kiss her, he'd have to do it in the next three blocks.

"I'm glad it stopped snowing," he said.

Laura laughed as if he had made a joke. "Me too!"

They came to a halt at a traffic stop. It occurred

to Sam that this was a perfect opportunity to make his move, but just then the light turned green. They trudged on wearily through the night.

Laura reached into her pocket for some mints and realized with panic that she'd left them at the bar. Her breath was almost certainly terrible.

Sam was also thinking about his breath. There was a pack of gum inside his coat. But in which pocket? He was debating whether or not to search for it when he realized they were already at his apartment.

"Is this your place?" Laura asked.

"Yeah," Sam said, pointing stupidly at the number on his awning. "Ninety-three Ludlow!"

He could feel a few cold drops of sweat stabbing through the pores in his armpits. Before going out, he had made his bed for the first time in weeks, on the off chance that he might somehow convince Laura to come back to his apartment. He couldn't face that bed alone, with its absurdly folded blanket and painstakingly fluffed pillows. It would be too much to bear. He had to at least kiss her, or he would never forgive himself. The conditions were perfect: a breeze in the air, a moon overhead—there was no excuse to fail.

But then he thought about how drunk he was and wondered if he was imagining things. What if Laura's flirtatious grin was merely a polite smile? What if he swooped in for a kiss and she started to laugh—or recoiled in disgust! If the kiss was unwanted, she could technically charge him with assault. That was unlikely, he realized, but fully within her rights as a woman. It didn't seem worth the risk.

"Well, hey," he stalled. "It was really cool hanging out with you."

"Yeah," Laura said. "I had a great time."

She thought about grabbing his face and pulling it down to hers, but she'd never done anything like that before. Besides, it was increasingly clear he wasn't interested in her. If he were, he would have made a move by now.

"So," she said, "I guess...I'll see ya?"

"Yeah!" he said. "Yeah...I'll see ya."

They shook hands stiffly and went their separate ways. They were both disappointed, but only slightly. After all, it was just one night. They'd have other chances. It wasn't the end of the world.

Craig stared numbly at the screen as the humans parted ways. Vince patted him on the shoulder and rose to his feet.

"Well, fellas," he said. "It was nice working with you."

"Where are you going?" Eliza asked him.

"The party," Vince said. "It sounds like a real rager."

He took off his pants and headed for the break room.

Eliza sat in her swivel chair and sidled up to Craig.

"There's still forty minutes left," she told him. "That's enough time to try something."

Craig shook his head, his eyes fixed on the screen. "It's hopeless."

Eliza raised her eyebrows in disbelief. "I never thought I'd hear you say that."

Craig shrugged. "Me neither."

She was about to squeeze his shoulder when a crashing noise distracted her.

"Oh no," she whispered. "Look."

She pointed down the hall. God was wobbling out of the bathroom, trying to find his way back to the party. Craig averted his eyes; he was in no mood for a conversation with his boss. But the old man quickly spotted him and came over to say hello.

"Big day tomorrow!" he said. "You as jazzed as I am?"

Craig nodded wearily.

"We're starting a restaurant," God proudly told Eliza.

"I've heard," she said.

"Let's see what you guys are working on," God mumbled, throwing his arms around them for support.

"Oh!" he said, peering at the screen. "That thing."

He shook his head and laughed. "Why do you guys work so hard? What's that *about?*"

Eliza shrugged. "We like doing it."

God smiled, genuinely moved.

"You know what?" he said. "You're good people."

"I guess that makes sense," Eliza said. "We got into heaven, right?"

God squinted at her, confused. "What do you mean?"

Eliza shrugged. "Just, you know, you picked us to get into heaven. So we must be good people."

God laughed. "That's not what it's based on."

"It's not?"

"Nah."

"So...what is it?" Craig asked. "What're the criteria?"

"You guys don't know?"

"Just tell us," Eliza said.

God smiled. "It's rock skipping."

Craig and Eliza nodded, waiting for God to elaborate. But he didn't seem to think he needed to.

"What are you talking about?" Craig asked eventually.

"You've got to get seven skips," God explained. "On any one throw."

Eliza turned pale. "That's it? Just skip a rock seven times and you're in? That's *all?*"

"What do you mean, 'that's all'?" God said. "Rock skipping is hard. Almost no one gets to seven skips."

"Seven skips," Craig repeated in a dazed monotone. "Unbelievable."

"Well, for women it's five," God said. "You know, so it's fair. They've got weaker arms."

Craig shook his head, stunned. "Why didn't you base it on something *important?*"

God stared at him blankly. "Like what?"

"I don't know. Like, righteousness? Or courage, or faith..."

"I thought about making it something like that," God said. "But those things are too hard to measure. Like, how can you tell how righteous someone is? It's not something you can just add up. With rock skipping, though, you can be like, 'Hey, that was four skips.' Or 'That was eight skips.' It works."

"What about disabled people?" Eliza asked. "They're just fucked?"

God shook his head. "Wheelchair people can skip rocks," he said. "Maybe it's a little harder for them to get leverage, but I've seen some make it work."

"What about landlocked people?" Craig asked. "People who live in places without water—like Nepal or New Mexico?"

God thought about that for a moment.

"They're fucked," he admitted.

In the distance, the opening chords of "Free Bird" blared through a giant loudspeaker.

"Oh, man!" he said. "That's my jam. I gotta go."

He bounded toward the break room.

"See you at Sola, Greg!"

Craig and Eliza didn't speak for a few minutes. Eventually, their silence was interrupted by a beeping sound.

Eliza smiled bitterly.

"Look," she said, pointing at Craig's monitor. "A Potential Miracle in Miami."

Craig did not respond.

"Hey, listen," she said. "I'm sorry things didn't work out. But at least you tried. That took real confidence."

Craig started to thank her, but the words got caught in his throat.

"Well, anyway," she said. "It was really nice working with you."

She awkwardly thrust out her hand; he shook it.

Craig watched in silence as she packed her bag and headed toward the elevators. Then he turned back toward his computer. He was about to turn it off when he stopped himself. There was still about half an hour left. He might as well enjoy it.

EARTH—THIRTY-SIX MINUTES UNTIL DOOMSDAY

Beto Lloreda Jr. sat in the right-field stands, working the bottom of a jumbo-sized Cracker Jack box. The Marlins were trailing 12–4 in the seventh, and his father was clamoring for them to leave so they could beat the postgame traffic. Beto stood on his chair to get one last good look at the field. Miami was down to its final strike of the inning, with no runners on and the pitcher up to bat.

"Come on," Beto Sr. said, snapping his fingers impatiently. "Come *on*."

Beto Jr. reluctantly took his dad's hand. His Marlins jersey, caked with sticky crumbs, hung down past his knees.

"Can I bring the Cracker Jacks?"

Beto Sr. shook his head. "It'll make a mess in the car."

The boy hung his head in disappointment. He was rooting around for a final handful when he heard the crack of a bat, followed by a rising commotion all around him.

"Look out!" someone shouted. "Kid, look out!"

He tilted his head up and watched in shock as the foul ball hooked wildly toward him. For a moment he stood motionless, too frightened to move an inch. But a second before contact, his instincts kicked in and he held the box up to shield his face. He closed his eyes, bracing himself for injury. He heard a muffled thud—then an eerie silence. When he finally opened his eyes, the stadium erupted in applause.

Beto reached into his Cracker Jack box and pulled out the baseball, still warm from its collision with the bat. Then he stood on his chair, held it above his head, and basked in the cheers of thousands.

Craig watched as Beto Sr. lifted his son onto his shoulders and carried the young hero out of the stadium. The Jumbotron broadcast their entire exit, even after the game resumed and the pitcher popped out to center field.

Craig laughed out loud as the Lloredas made their way to the parking lot, slapping strangers' hands and posing for the occasional picture. They were almost at their car when Craig reached for the power switch.

"See ya," he whispered.

He closed his eyes as the screen went black.

Part III

EARTH—TWENTY-FIVE MINUTES UNTIL DOOMSDAY

"IS IT TOO LATE?" SAM demanded, his voice thick with anguish. "Please, tell me it's not too late."

There was dead silence on the other line. Sam closed his eyes, bracing himself for rejection.

"I know I made a mistake," he continued. "I waited too long. I'm sorry—really, really sorry. I just…it would be so amazing if you could come over."

"Apologize first," Raj demanded. "Apologize for calling so late."

"I apologize!" Sam cried earnestly. "I lost track of time."

Raj hesitated. "I have no puri left—only naan."

"That's fine," Sam assured him. "I'll take anything!"

"Okay," Raj said. "I'll be there in ten minutes."

Sam thanked him profusely and hung up the phone, relieved that the night's crisis had been averted.

Laura was taking off her jeans when she felt her cell phone vibrate. She rummaged through her pocket, hoping it was Sam—a text message, maybe, wishing her good-night. But it was just an unknown number with a Staten Island area code.

"I win the prize?" an older man asked her.

"Which prize?" she answered, her voice soft with disappointment.

"Jets tickets."

Laura looked at her cell phone. It was 11:41 p.m. She thought about sending Sam a text saying she'd had fun. But what would that accomplish? Besides, he was probably asleep by now. She didn't want to wake him up.

"Hello?" the man said. "Lady?"

She glimpsed her reflection in her laptop, and the sight was so humiliating she had to close her computer. She hadn't worn makeup for weeks until today and the sight of her rouged cheeks made her cringe. There was nothing more depressing than wasted cosmetics.

"Lady?" the man repeated.

"No," she whispered. Her voice was so small the man couldn't hear her.

"What?"

"No," she said. "You lost. In fact, the contest is over."

"Really?"

"Yes, we're not doing the prizes anymore, so you can stop calling. I'm sorry to tell you this, I just don't want you to get your hopes up anymore. There aren't any more prizes."

"Jesus. Lady, are you okay?"

Laura realized with shock that she was crying.

"Honey," the man said, in as gentle a voice as he could muster. "It's no big deal. I don't even like the Jets."

"I'm really sorry," she repeated, before turning off her phone. "See ya."

"Is not healthy," Raj warned as he counted out Sam's change. "One dinner should be enough for one man."

"This is my first dinner," Sam said. "Actually—it's my first meal all day. If you don't count bar nuts."

Raj crinkled his massive eyebrows. "Bar?"

Sam blushed. "Yeah," he murmured. "I went on a date. Well, you know, it was just going to be coffee. But it kind of turned into a date. I think."

For the first time in their relationship, Raj's lips curled into a smile.

"Describe the girl."

"Come on, Raj..."

He reached for his dinner—and Raj pulled the bag out of reach.

"*Describe* her," he commanded.

Sam reluctantly told him about Laura—how they'd met, how he'd run into her at the Apple Store, how they'd danced and laughed and almost kissed.

"I really like her," he said.

"And how does she respond?" Raj demanded, his voice loud and resonant. "When you make your advances?"

Sam laughed. "I don't know," he said. "I've never exactly made an 'advance.'"

"Do it now."

Sam laughed again and reached for his food. Raj yanked the bag out of reach.

"You love this girl," he said. "Admit this."

Sam sighed.

"Okay," he said. "I admit it."

"Then you must make an advance," Raj said. "Or else I will not serve you."

Sam clenched his fists and stamped his right foot like a frustrated child.

"This isn't funny," he cried. "I'm *really* hungry."

Raj's eyes narrowed. "My mind is stone."

Sam threw up his hands in frustration. "Fine!" he said. "Fine. I'll send her a text."

"What is 'text'?" Raj asked, spitting out the unfamiliar word with disgust.

"It's how people communicate now."

"Is not how a *man* communicates."

"Okay," Sam muttered. "Jesus! I'll call her. I'll ask her if she wants to go out again."

"That is not good enough."

Sam took a swipe at Raj's bag, and Raj slapped his palm with a surprising amount of force.

"You must do it in person."

"She's probably asleep by now!"

"You must try. Or else no food. No vindaloo, no naan..." His eyes narrowed. "No sauces, green or red."

Sam shook his head wearily. He was so weak from hunger he could barely keep his head up, and his brain was still foggy from all the gin.

"I'm not even wearing pants."

Raj folded his arms and squinted. "It is time to put them on!"

Sam staggered up Ludlow, buckling his pants as he walked. After a few minutes of rigorous debate, he'd agreed on a compromise with Raj. He'd walk to Laura's awning and send her a text message. ("It's like a telegram," he'd insisted to Raj.) If Laura was still awake, he'd ask her to come downstairs and say hello. Otherwise, he'd walk straight home. Either way, the food was complimentary, along with two complimentary servings of garlic naan for his efforts.

It was such a short walk he hadn't bothered to put on

his coat. But as he trudged through the October night, he began to regret his decision. The light snowfall—already odd for this time of year—had escalated into another blizzard. He paused to look up at the sky. The snow was tumbling down in sheets.

Sam considered bailing. According to his phone, it was 11:57 p.m.—which meant he'd been walking for a good five minutes. If he turned back now, Raj would have no reason to believe he hadn't made it all the way to Laura's.

There was only one problem with that plan: Raj would never believe him. He'd never successfully lied to him in his life. Sam took a deep breath and trudged onward, shielding his face with his forearm.

Laura sat by her window, taking off her makeup. She was relieved it was almost midnight. A new episode of *Bizarre Bodies* was about to premiere.

She was on her way over to the couch when she heard a thump against her window. She assumed it was a piece of hail, but a second thump convinced her to peek outside. A man stood shivering beneath her awning, caked with snow, tossing clumps of ice against her window. She was thinking about calling the police when she caught sight of Sam's face beneath a streetlight. He waved at her awkwardly, and she ran down the stairs to the door. It was 11:58 p.m.

* * *

"Your phone was off," Sam explained, his voice shaky from the cold. "But I saw you in the window…so…I threw ice."

"What are you doing on my street?" she asked.

"Raj said I had to," he sputtered through chattering teeth. "For dinner."

"What?"

Sam cleared his throat. "I never bought you dinner!" he said, recovering. He had to shout to be heard over the howling wind.

"Oh!" she said, laughing. "You don't have to! I mean, unless you want to."

"Well, it's not a date without dinner."

She smiled self-consciously. "Was that…were we on a date?"

Sam looked down at his feet. "I don't know, were we?"

A thunderclap sounded in the distance, followed by the crunching collapse of a snow-laden tree. Sam noticed that Laura's teeth had begun to chatter, just like his. He instinctively rubbed her shoulder, trying to protect her from the cold. She grabbed his hand and blew on it, warming it with her breath. His thumb brushed against her lips, and she held it there for a moment. When she exhaled, he could see her breath through his fingers.

"Sorry to keep you up so late," he whispered.

"It's not that late," she said. "It's not even midnight."

She squeezed his hand, and for the first time in his entire life he looked directly into her eyes.

"I like you," he said.

She laughed. "I like you too."

"No, I mean..." He looked around helplessly. "What I mean is..."

A series of thunderclaps sounded, one after the other, and the blizzard suddenly intensified. The awning began to creak, straining under the weight of fallen snow.

Sam closed his eyes, still searching for the right phrase. He was about to open them when he felt Laura's lips on his. He tentatively kissed her and, with some anxiety, opened his eyes.

They laughed awkwardly—then kissed again, less fearfully this time, Laura's tongue probing bravely through Sam's parted lips.

Sam took a deep, slow breath. There was something he desperately wanted to ask her, but he feared what her response might be.

"Laura?" he whispered. "Do you like Indian food?"

"I *love* it," she said, her eyes bright with intensity.

Sam was so relieved he kissed her again.

"Let's get some," he said. "Right now."

"Is anyplace open?"

"Not exactly," Sam said, debonairly. "But I'm kind of a big deal over at Bombay Palace."

"We could get takeout and watch *Bizarre Bodies*!" Laura blurted. She was immediately embarrassed, but Sam was already nodding and taking her hand. At some point, it had stopped snowing. The humans marched proudly down the avenue.

It was 12:01 a.m., a whole new day.

Epilogue

"I'M NOT MAKING NEW SIGNS," Raoul said.

"You don't have to," God promised. "The world's not going to end anymore."

Raoul groaned and rubbed his naked stomach. He was lying in the middle of a golf course, surrounded by empty bottles of MD 20/20.

"You should've told me yesterday," he complained. "If I knew I was going to live till morning, I never would've hit that Taco Bell so hard."

He wearily shook his head. "I ate bad things."

God nodded sympathetically. "That's on me," he said. "I had to change my plans at the last second."

"Why?"

"I lost a bet."

Raoul nodded, satisfied with the explanation.

"I'm sorry, Raoul. It must be miserable having to stay down there."

Raoul shrugged. "It's not so bad. I kind of like it."

"Really?"

"Yeah, it's a good planet. You know what I like? The fruit."

God blushed. "The fruit was my idea."

Raoul nodded. "Thank you."

God smiled cheerfully. "You're welcome!"

He kicked his feet up on the desk and laughed. Maybe Raoul was right? Maybe Earth wasn't as worthless as he thought? He'd never expected those losers in New York to hook up. But just as he was about to give his demolition order, Vince had drunkenly asked him to check on the two humans one last time. God almost choked on a nacho when he saw them sucking face in the middle of a sidewalk. It was a sloppy kiss—but a kiss all the same—and God had no choice but to call off the planet's destruction. Part of him was disappointed, but another part was secretly relieved. There was a lot about mankind he would've missed.

"You know what?" he told Raoul. "I've got a message for the humans after all."

Raoul whipped a Sharpie out of his underwear. "I'm on it."

"I want you to make a big sign, your biggest one yet. And I want it to say, 'God Loves You.'"

"That's it?"

God nodded firmly. "That's it."

He smiled as his prophet copied the phrase onto a flattened cardboard box.

"I'll wave this in people's faces," Raoul said. "And, you know, scream at them and stuff."

"That's great," God said. "You're the best."

Out of the corner of his eye, he noticed his Rubik's Cube, still lying in his wooden wastebasket.

He hesitated for a moment, then grabbed it.

"I can't believe it," Craig said to Vince. "Angel of the Month!"

"You deserve it," Vince said. "That foul-ball miracle was really something."

Craig thanked him and greedily opened his prize. A coupon fluttered out of the envelope, landing on his desk. He picked it up and read the text out loud.

"One half-price appetizer at Sola with the purchase of two entrées."

He turned the coupon over and squinted at the fine print.

"'Limit one per customer...meat appetizers excluded...expires in twenty-four hours.'"

He shrugged. "Guess I'll go tonight?"

Vince laughed and unpacked his stapler. God had offered him a job managing reservations at Sola, but he'd turned it down. It's not that he bore any ill will toward his boss; he was just sick of working with the guy. He wanted to do something challenging—something that mattered to him. He'd asked God if he could take over as CEO of Heaven Inc., but the old man wanted to keep the position, even if it was just an honorary title. After some thought, Vince decided to do the next best thing. He demoted himself to Angel and rejoined the Miracles Department. He was taking over Brian's old cubicle, just a few steps away from Craig.

"Holy shit," he muttered, as he opened the filing cabinet. "This whole thing is full of bottles."

Craig nodded. "Brian had a bad problem." He shook his head wistfully. "I wonder where he is now."

Vince cocked his head. "You haven't heard? God promoted him to Archangel."

"Seriously?"

"Yeah. Apparently they really bonded at that End of the World party. You'll probably see him at Sola. He's got a regular spot at the bar."

Craig smiled. "Good for him. Hey, do you want to come with me tonight? I don't think I can eat two whole entrées by myself."

Vince chuckled. "You're asking *me?*"

"Who else should I ask?"

Vince gestured subtly toward Eliza's cubicle. She was hunched over her computer, finishing up a fishing miracle. Vince handed the coupon to Craig and nodded. "Don't blow it."

* * *

"Hey, congrats!" Eliza said. "That sounds like a pretty good prize."

"Yeah, I know!" Craig said. "I mean, you know, it's nothing to sneeze at." He toed the carpet. "Anyway, I was wondering..." He looked around helplessly. "Uh...I was wondering if maybe you'd like to grab coffee sometime?"

She smiled gently at him. "Grab coffee?"

He looked down at his feet. "I mean..." He cleared his throat and looked into her eyes. "I mean, do you want to go on a date with me?"

She nodded. "That sounds like fun."

He sighed gigantically. "Great! That's great. So... when do you want to leave work?"

"How about right now?"

Craig laughed. "We can't go *now*. I mean, look at Sam and Laura."

He gestured at his screen: the two humans were sitting alone in their apartments, staring at their iPhones, each one waiting for the other to call.

"What if they screw it up?" Craig said. "What if they both chicken out and never call each other? What if, after everything we've done for them, they still manage to ruin it?"

Eliza shrugged. "It's in their hands now."

Craig looked into her eyes and smiled.

"You're right," he said, reaching for the off switch. "It's in their hands."

Acknowledgments

I first read the Bible in 1997, when I was studying for my bar mitzvah. It scared me so much that I pledged to keep kosher for the rest of my life. I kept the vow for nearly three days, when I accidentally ate a full rack of ribs. Since then, on some level, I've been waiting for God to kill me.

I want to thank Central Synagogue Hebrew School for forcing me to study Torah. They failed to turn me into an observant Jew, but they succeeded in turning me into a comedy writer.

My family also deserves a lot of the credit. I want to thank my mom (for letting me watch five episodes of *The Simpsons* every day for ten years); my dad (for buying me two separate Neil Simon anthologies when

I was twelve); my stepmom, Alex (for getting me my first subscription to *Mad* magazine); Michael (for giving me *Catch-22*); Nat (for letting me steal the Philip Roth novels off his shelf); and my hilarious Grandma Nita (who introduced me to the phrase "What in God's name!").

Daniel Greenberg believed in this novel when nobody else did (including me). If it weren't for his support and advice, there's no way this book would exist.

Reagan Arthur drastically improved these pages with her shrewd critiques and brilliant suggestions.

Susan Morrison, my editor at *The New Yorker,* once casually suggested over lunch that I write a novel about God. I'm not sure if she remembers saying that. Anyway, Susan, here it is, five years later. Thanks for the idea!

I want to thank Lee Eastman, Patricia O'Hearn, Gregory McKnight, and everyone else at Allagash Industries for believing in all my crazy projects. I don't know how I would survive without you.

And I want to thank Professor Kimberley C. Patton at Harvard Divinity School, whose fascinating courses first inspired me to write about angels.

Jake Luce, as usual, helped me enormously at every stage of the writing process. The day he stops reading my drafts is the day I stop writing books.

Thanks also to Dustin Lushing, Amelia Gonzalez, Marika Sawyer, John Mulaney, Seth Meyers, Lorne

Michaels, Steve Higgins, Andrew Singer, Marlena Bittner, Sarah Murphy, Rebecca Gray, Anna-Marie Fitzgerald, Kathleen Hale, Peg Anderson, Melissa Fuller, Deborah Jacobs, Laura Tisdel, Peggy Leith Anderson, Montague Wines and Spirits, Pixar, and Tabasco sauce. You all helped in your own way.

Thanks to all my friends for putting up with me.

And thanks, above all, to my wonderful big brother Nat, who taught me everything I know about books, life, and baseball. This one's for you.

About the Author

Simon Rich is the author of *Spoiled Brats, Man Seeking Woman, Miracle Workers, Ant Farm, Free-Range Chickens,* and *Elliot Allagash*. He has written for *Saturday Night Live,* Pixar, and *The Simpsons,* and he is the creator and showrunner of *Man Seeking Woman* and *Miracle Workers,* both of which he based on his books. His work appears frequently in *The New Yorker*. He lives in Los Angeles.

BACK BAY · READERS' PICK

Reading Group Guide

Miracle Workers

A Novel

Simon Rich

An interview with Simon Rich

Simon Rich begins his novel *Miracle Workers* with a verse from Genesis 1:27, "So God created man in his own image..." That ellipsis is what sets Rich apart from just about every other American comedy writer today: he's able to mine even the oldest and most familiar sources for material that feels revelatory and exciting. *Miracle Workers* is an often hilarious examination of what it would mean for God to be like humans, *really* like us. In Rich's second novel, God is the uninterested CEO of a holy corporation whose real passion is opening an Asian-fusion restaurant and who created life on Earth while procrastinating. One of the most memorable sequences involves Vince, an archangel, explaining that all human choices can be explained by "what they had eaten for breakfast, whether or not they had slept well, and how long it had been since their last satisfactory orgasm." Whatever he's eating for breakfast, Rich's choices seem to have worked out remarkably well. He went straight from the *Harvard Lampoon* to being the youngest writer hired on *Saturday Night Live*. He's a frequent contributor to *The New Yorker* and has written for Pixar. *Wag's Revue* contributor Chris Duffy spoke with Simon on the phone.

Where do you get the ideas for your humor premises?

The World Book Encyclopedia and Wikipedia are huge influences on my writing. I click the random article button to see what comes up. When I was writing *Ant Farm,* a big thing I would do is go to the library, and they have bound volumes of old *Life* magazines, and I would just go through page by page until I saw something that triggered a premise.

I read a lot of nonfiction. I read a lot of books about weird historical figures like Ivan the Terrible and Caligula and strange historical time periods like the Dark Ages. I read a lot of *Popular Science* about robots and monkeys and early human history. I love big old books like *Grimm's Fairy Tales* and the Bible and cultural histories of America. These are the subjects I'm obsessed with.

If you can't come up with comedy premises based on subjects as interesting as those, then you're in trouble. I also obviously draw from my own life and my own experience, but that has always been my secret weapon, reading a lot of nonfiction.

Your father is Frank Rich and your brother is a novelist as well. How much does coming from a family of writers help you?

A lot. I never had the experience of having to convince my family that writing was an acceptable job. So many of my friends who are writers have colossally let their families down. Especially at a place like the *Harvard Lampoon,* most of the people on staff have families that expect them to come to school to be doctors or engineers, something with merit, but I had already announced to my parents at a very young age that I was going to pick this frivolous profession and they always supported me. That's the main leg up I had, I think: having parents who were completely accepting of my choice to be a writer, which is rare.

At Saturday Night Live, *you often wrote in a team with Marika Sawyer and John Mulaney. Marika is one of the longest-tenured female writers on the show and John is a top-tier stand-up comic. How did you all first start working together?*

We were all hired at *SNL* at around the same time. It happened really naturally; we just found each other and realized we were writing really similar sorts of pieces. We teamed up on a couple of sketches and had a great time and decided to keep doing it. We wrote basically every week together for a couple of years. Writing with them was by far the best part of *SNL* for me.

What makes a comedy writer successful?

I've seen all different types of paths to success. At *SNL,* there were people who had come from the *Lampoon* but there were also people who had been stand-up comedians, who had been improvisers, who had been in sketch comedy troupes, people who considered themselves actors until the moment they became writers at *SNL.* All these people were enormously talented. I don't think there is a set path.

Is that different for performers? It seems like there's a pretty clear career path for comedians to get on SNL. *You perform at UCB in New York or Second City in Chicago, you make a bunch of comedy videos for YouTube, and then you get lucky and Lorne Michaels picks you.*

That's mostly true but there are also exceptions to that. If you look at Marika and Mulaney, Mulaney had been doing stand-up comedy and was asked to audition for the cast of *SNL.* His material was so good they hired him to be a writer. And Marika had been a receptionist at *SNL* after being an intern for a number of years. Receptionists are allowed to submit jokes to Weekend Update and she sold some jokes and they read her packet and it was fantastic.

One of the characters in your book, Vince, says that almost all human choices are based on "what they had eaten for breakfast, whether or not they had slept well, and how long it had been since their last satisfactory orgasm." How much of that is your opinion?

Vince is obviously a pretty cynical character. But I've always been interested in the extent to which we're controlled by our biological impulses. That's something that a lot of my favorite writers talk about, guys like T. C. Boyle especially.

I think it's hilarious how much of our lives is determined by something as base as our need to procreate or make money or things like that. With Vince, I tried to create someone who would espouse an extreme version of that philosophy. I thought that would make for a good villain.

It's interesting that you brought up cynicism, because your writing frequently explores religion and the sacred but manages to avoid crossing the line into the cynical or profane. It seems like even when you poke fun at religion, you're approaching it from a respectful and almost scholarly angle.

Well, thanks, I appreciate that. I don't consider myself a cynical person and I think I've gotten a lot less cynical as my career has progressed. The original title for my first book was *Horrible Situations* and the original ending was a short piece, which I cut, which was a conversation with a time traveler where the time traveler shows up and just tells me to kill myself. That's the entire piece.

When I was writing those pieces, I was a teenager. I had a lot of angst, the typical existential angst that teenagers have. I don't know, I'm twenty-eight now. By the time I wrote *Miracle Workers* my life had changed a lot. I wasn't a scared sad teenager anymore. I was a grown-up person who had fallen in love, who had experienced a lot of wonderful things in my life. I'm not consciously trying to write redemptive books or uplifting stories, but as someone who's ultimately pretty earnest and optimistic, my books kind of take on that color.

You don't seem to use comedy as therapy. I'm always frustrated by the idea that to be a successful comedian you have to be emotionally damaged.

I think that's a really good point. I think that even when I was a teenager, my funniest pieces were not the ones where I was angry. That's not to say that there aren't funny comedians who are angry, but to this day all of my favorite comedy writers, all of my favorite humorists, have been pretty universal and accessible and very few of them write from a place of anger.

Guys like David Sedaris or Roald Dahl, they're not satirists, they're not nasty critics laying into different aspects of society. They're writing about funny traits that a lot of humans have in common.

Who are some other writers that you like?

I like writers who come up with good hooks and good premises, and it doesn't necessarily matter to me if they're funny. For example, I really like Stephen King, I really like Jerzy Kosinski. Kosinski, if you read a book like *Cockpit* or *Blind Date,* it's just one hook after the other. It keeps ensnaring you.

There's also an aspect to those books where the horror premise could easily become comedy if written by someone else.

Oh yeah, it's a very thin line. A huge influence on me has been *The Twilight Zone,* and I think *The Simpsons* has shown, with its Halloween episodes, that there's almost no line between horror and comedy. Regardless of genre, my favorite writers are the ones who give you a strong hooky premise. For me, that's what I'm aspiring to do every time I sit down and write. What's a way I can hook the reader and make them keep reading until I can hook them again?

You once said that your favorite perspective to write from is "any perspective where someone is missing some vital piece of information—preferably a piece of information so vital that it will probably result in their death." Does that still ring true?

Oh yeah. I mean, look, that's my only gimmick. I'm not going to abandon it unless I come up with another one.

The other thing, as a writer, at least for me, is I'm always trying to raise the stakes as much as possible. Because that's a cheap way to make the story more interesting. Like, I could have written a novel about two people who needed to kiss otherwise they...won't...date? But instead I decided to write a novel about two people who need to kiss and if they don't the world will explode. For me, that's just more interesting.

What is your own relationship to God and spirituality?

Ever since I went to Hebrew school and read the Old Testament, I've been really interested in religion and interested in the character of God in particular. When I first read the Torah, I was twelve years old and I couldn't believe how irrational and crazy God was. I mean, the first time he speaks to Abraham he asks him to cut off part of his penis. And then to cut off parts of all his male servants' penises. Abraham is ninety-nine years old and he has no choice but to do this crazy thing.

I think God is a pretty wacky character. He's constantly destroying the Earth with floods or fires, but he also bargains with Abraham about whether or not he's going to go through with his acts of destruction. He tells Abraham he's got to murder his own son and then sends an angel to call it off at the last second. He's just testing to make sure that Abraham loves him. I mean, that's such a needy, passive-aggressive, vulnerable thing to do, to test Abraham to see if he would kill his son for you. So I always thought he was a fascinating, fascinating character.

I remember in seventh grade, I went to at least two bar mitzvahs every weekend. It always struck me that some kids get lucky and their Torah portion is actually meaningful, but other kids end up with a really esoteric passage with, like, instructions on how to feed your goats.

Right, right, right! And then they have to give a speech about it. My Torah portion was an incredibly dull list of names. I mean, the Old Testament is full of incredibly boring passages, but I think mine was easily top ten most boring passages. Literally it was the results of the first Jewish census. And I had to expound in front of my friends and family for ten minutes about why God had decided to dictate this.

Do you see the character Sam as a version of yourself?

When I'm writing fiction, I see every single character, including the ones that are mostly evil, as a version of myself. I think it would be impossible to write a character that I had nothing in common with. I don't know how I would do that.

How I come up with characters is I take an emotion that I've had or a way I've been and heighten it to the point that it becomes its own streamlined version of myself. I actually don't know if that's how other writers do it, but that's how I have always done it.

The original version of this interview appeared in the online literary quarterly *Wag's Revue,* available at wagsrevue.com.

Five questions about *Miracle Workers*

1. The premise behind *Miracle Workers* is a grim one, yet the humor is warm and the tone and characters optimistic. How would your reading experience have been different if the humor had been dark or sardonic?

2. The deal that Craig and Eliza strike with God is that they'll fulfill one earthly prayer in a month. What, in the context of the book, does fulfilling a prayer entail? What is the novel saying about human nature, desire, or the subconscious mind by making a human prayer so hard to answer?

3. Many novels that center on religion do so to criticize or satirize anti-intellectualism. Is that part of the agenda here? If not, why choose religion as the vehicle for wit?

4. In an interview about this novel in *The Rumpus,* Simon Rich said, "Throughout my childhood, teachers urged me to fight the establishment. My English teacher assigned Ginsberg and Kerouac and declared

Bob Dylan 'a genius.' My science teacher told me that television was 'the new opiate of the masses.' But I didn't share their hatred of the establishment. After all, the establishment had given me so many of my favorite things: Nick at Nite, the New York Knicks, Stephen King, Taco Bell, Green Day." Yet *Miracle Workers* is at least broadly about a mismanaged, semi-heartless corporation. Are Rich's comments at odds with the themes of this novel? How is this satirical send-up different from being "anti-establishment"?

5. At one point in the book, after Craig rigs a wrestling match, he wonders, "Was it still a miracle if someone has to suffer?" What role does human suffering play in the novel? Ultimately, would Craig and Eliza consider this early miracle to have been actually miraculous? What are we, as readers, meant to learn from that question?

Five books that inspired *Miracle Workers*

The Hitchhiker's Guide to the Galaxy, by Douglas Adams

Good Omens, by Neil Gaiman and Terry Pratchett

Catch-22, by Joseph Heller

The Dilbert Principle, by Scott Adams

The Book of Genesis

Five books to read after *Miracle Workers*

The Magic Christian, by Terry Southern

Descent of Man, by T. C. Boyle

Tales of the Unexpected, by Roald Dahl

Et Tu, Babe, by Mark Leyner

Boxer, Beetle, by Ned Beauman